The Janus Gate

The Janus Gate

An Encounter with John Singer Sargent

DOUGLAS REES

WATSON-GUPTILL PUBLICATIONS/NEW YORK

Acknowledgements

I wish to thank Erica Hirshler of the Boston Museum of Fine Arts for providing information from their files
from their files on John Singer Sargent and the painting of "The Daughters of Edward Darley Boit."

Series Editor: Jacqueline Ching
Editor: Laaren Brown
Production Manager: Hector Campbell
Book Design: Jennifer Browne

First published in 2006 in the United States by Watson-Guptill Publications,
a division of VNU Business Media, Inc.,
770 Broadway, New York, NY 10003
www.wgpub.com

Front cover: John Singer Sargent, American, 1856-1925, *The Daughters of Edward Darley Boit* (1882). Oil on canvas, 221.93 x 222.57 cm (87 3/8 x 87 5/8in). Gift of Mary Louisa Boit, Julia Overing Boit, Jane Hubbard Boit, and Florence D. Boit, in memory of their father, Edward Darley Boit 19.124. Courtesy of the Museum of Fine Arts, Boston.

Library of Congress Cataloging-in-Publication Data
Rees, Douglas.
The Janus gate : an encounter with John Singer Sargent / by Douglas Rees.
p. cm.—(Art encounters)
Summary: Hired to paint a family portrait of four beautiful but mysterious daughters
in late nineteenth-century Paris, artist John Singer Sargent enters a world populated by
an emotionally unstable mother, a strange spirit, and a malevolent doll.
ISBN 0-8230-0406-6
1. Sargent, John Singer, 1856-1925—Juvenile fiction.   [1. Sargent, John Singer, 1856-1925—Fiction.
2. Artists—Fiction.   3. Dolls—Fiction.   4. Spirits—Fiction.   5. Paris (France)—Fiction.]   I. Title.   II. Series.
PZ7.R25475Ja 2006   [Fic]—dc22   2005028878

This book was set in Stempel Garamond.

Printed in the U.S.A.
First printing, 2006

1   2   3   4   5   6   7   /   12   11   10   09   08   07   06

To Laaren

Contents

My Dear H.J.,

Last Christmas Eve you asked us all to share ghost stories. As I recall, your precise words were: "Let us each tell something true, or at least not knowingly false, and preferably something that suggests the flexibility, or perhaps more accurately the tenuousness, of the nature of reality."

I was not quite sure what you meant, my friend, so when it came to be my turn, I could offer only a short and incomplete version of what you have before you now.

"Perhaps it's a ghost story and perhaps it isn't," I'd said at the time. "But it is certainly the strangest thing that has ever happened to me."

Since then you have asked me more than once for a more complete account. These pages are all I can remember. Some years have passed, and there may be a few details that I have recalled inexactly, or things I have left out that you would prefer to have had me write.

I was most reluctant to begin this. Words have power, and written words may have power that goes on for ages. Nonetheless, I find myself grateful to you now that it's finished. Perhaps I can begin to forget these things.

But no, that is not possible.

First Impressions

I have always been a man of first impressions. They strike me like bursts of light and overwhelm me, reducing me to silence, or to stuttering, telegraphic speech. I wave my hands and try to say something such as, "This painting of Millet's is far too realistic for my taste. See how he has tried to get the absolute reality of every inch of the surface of these rocks, every leaf of these trees. Of course that can't be done. Paint is paint and reality is reality."

But what comes out is "Millet—all those rocks and trees. Silly old thing," while my hands go like signal flags on a naval ship in the middle of a battle.

My first impressions have this trait: They keep happening. No matter how long I know someone it seems that I am capable of being surprised, astonished by them again and again; and each of these moments has the quality of absolute newness and truth.

I paint portraits for my living. I am popular and well paid. "Get Sargent to do your picture," the owners of machine-gun factories and sugar mills will say to one another. "John Singer Sargent. American, but you wouldn't know it. Speaks with an English accent. Speaks French like a Frenchman. A gentleman to his fingertips. He's the right sort. Good? Of course he's good. Good, but not too good." What they mean is that, in addition to being a master of my craft—many painters are masters of the craft of portraits—I paint my subjects as they strike me in these moments of absolute clarity. Then I refine them so that they look beautiful.

These moments of clarity are not always pleasant; far from it. Sometimes I see things that the person buying the portrait would never want me to know. These things I soften—a little. Very well, sometimes a lot. I have painted greed and ignorance, and a great many times I have painted vanity. But I know how to make these things beautiful.

Only once have I painted horror.

2

Varnishing Day

Varnishing Day at the Salon is a hell only an artist can know. Thousands of paintings have been hung on the walls of the Palais d'Industrie, more than anyone can possibly see in one day. And for the unfortunate many who have been "skied"—hung near the ceilings—the prospects for being seen at all are dim.

Then the doors open and thousands of the most demanding and opinionated art lovers in existence attack this year's crop of paintings, armed with sneers that in some cases have been in their families for generations. The art public of Paris will leave hopes shredded and lives trodden underfoot in its search for the next great painter.

That Varnishing Day of 1880 I was twenty-three and had my first picture there. *Fumee d'Amber Gris* had a decent place on the wall, thank God. My beauty was hung now, her varnish was dry, and it was time to turn her over to the tender mercies of the art world.

I strolled past the many pictures, wishing all of them well, and stopped at the one I'd come especially to see. It was all the talk of the Salon that year, the inside favorite. The subject was perfectly ordinary, and the style was just slightly daring—a good candidate for a prize.

It was a huge, glossy, elegant thing that depicted a festival day in ancient Rome. The gates of the city were open, and a long line of girls, garlanded with flowers, were trouping through them. Standing in the shadows, almost lurking, were a cluster of ancient crones. They seemed about to enter the city. What gave the painting its slightly daring air was the angle of vision. The artist had managed to paint his scene in such a way that the two busts of Janus, facing inward and outward over the gates, dominated the picture. It was very clever. The title was *The Janus Gate*.

"Papa, where are all the girls going?"

The voice came from behind me and not much above waist level. A child's voice, an American voice. Surprised, I turned, and found myself staring into the face of a grotesque china doll as big as a baby.

The doll was in the arms of a beautiful child of about three. She herself was in the arms of her father. He was a man some years older than myself, very pleasant looking and extremely well dressed.

"Papa, where are the girls going?" the voice repeated.

I looked down, and almost gasped.

Tugging on the sleeve of her father was the most perfect child I had ever seen. She was perhaps six; and her pale skin, blonde hair, and dark blue eyes were somehow the emblems of childhood itself. And the way she looked up at her father, with perfect love and trust, pierced me with its truth. I am afraid I stared. I am beauty's fool.

The father shifted the child he was holding to free up one arm and gestured at the scene.

"They are going out into the countryside to celebrate the spring and their own youth," he said.

"But why are there two ugly goblins over their heads?" the little beauty asked.

"They're not goblins, Mary," the father said. "That is Janus, who guards the gates of Rome. He has two faces."

"If he's not a goblin, why does he have two heads?" Mary asked.

"There you have me," Father said. "I'm sure I was taught that in school, but I've forgotten it."

There was something about the three of them that I liked at once. A warmth that is rare between children and fathers, a quality of easy elegance. I wished to know more of them, and it made me bold.

"If I may," I said. Lessons were not very far in my past then; I remembered my Latin readings perfectly. Now if I could only explain them! "I—I—Janus—not only the guardian of Rome's gates—all entryways—way to the future and the past. So—two faces in opposite directions. See? The old women going the opposite way, looking back at—at youth and beauty."

At least my hand did not fly off the end of my arm as I wildly gestured.

"That's it exactly," the father said. "Thank you, sir."

"Forgive me," I said. "Intrusion, I know."

"Not at all, sir." The father smiled. "Very good of you. Thanks."

There was a thunder of feet coming toward us. The wall of art lovers was suddenly pierced by a trio of young harpies.

The tallest and oldest had each of her claws dug into the shoulders of the other two. Their governess, I guessed. A very prim mademoiselle she seemed, and at that moment she was furious. So were the other two, an almost matched pair of dark-haired beauties.

"Monsieur Boit," Mademoiselle hissed in French. "Your daughters are insufferable!"

"What have they done now, Mademoiselle?" Father Boit asked. He seemed as much amused as worried.

"We were only singing, Papa," said the younger girl, who was ten or eleven. "We were singing to the painting. It was singing to us."

"And what were you singing, eh, Mademoiselle Jane? Tell your father that," Mademoiselle demanded.

"Au prêt de ma blonde,
Qu'il fait bon, fait bon, fait bon.
Au prêt de ma blonde,
Qu'il fait bon, fait bon!"

Jane began. The older girl joined in, in perfect harmony.

I blushed, despite my best efforts to look worldly. The words, of course, are about being "near my dear one," but they are distinctly inappropriate for young ladies.

"Cease!" Mademoiselle said.

Father Boit laughed. He laughed so loudly that he had to muzzle himself with his free hand.

The passersby glared at this outburst, and they were right. It was a wholly improper song for young ladies, and laughter is never encouraged at the Salon—except at the expense of artists. Still, I could not help being further charmed. The girls were so natural, their father so delighted by their misdeed. Most fathers would not have been.

"Girls, you must not sing to the paintings," Father Boit said. "No matter how much they might seem to wish it. And you must never sing that song at all."

"But Papa, why not?" the older girl asked.

"That is the sort of answer that your mother can give you when you are a little older, Florence," Father Boit said. "Now, suppose you tell me to which painting you were singing."

"That great big one over there, Father," said Jane, pointing.

"Mademoiselle Jane, do not point. It is rude," said their governess.

"Yes, Mademoiselle," Jane said. "But it was that one."

And she pointed with her foot, lifting it like a ballerina.

"Jane," her father warned. "If you drive this mademoiselle off as you did the others, you will be sent away to school."

"For how long, Papa?" asked Jane. She seemed very concerned.

"Until you are forty-two," her father said.

Jane lowered her foot.

"Papa, you must not send Jane away," Florence implored. "I cannot exist without Jane."

The two girls clasped hands.

"I shall do so only if you force me to it," Father said. I turned away so the girls would not see my smile, and realized the painting they had sung to was mine. *Fumee d'Amber Gris* shows a beautiful North African woman standing before an incense burner at her feet. She is dressed in white and has a shawl spread above her head to concentrate the perfume she is inhaling.

"Oh, look," said Mr. Boit. "It must be the new Sargent. I see your point, girls. It sings to me, even from here." He sighed. "If I could paint like that . . ."

I blushed at the praise. I was curious too. In Paris almost all the American painters know each other, at least slightly. But I did not know this Mr. Boit.

"I beg your pardon," I said again. "Are you a painter? Do you have something here?"

Again my arm waved, taking in the Salon.

"Yes, I paint a little," Mr. Boit said. "Watercolors. I try to resemble Corot. But no, I have no painting here."

A Sunday painter then. No harm in that.

"Papa paints the most beautiful flowers in the world," said Jane. "They are very sad."

"Why is that?" I asked, charmed again. "If I were a flower, I think I'd be very happy about it."

"They are sad because they are not real and they want to be," said Florence.

"Mademoiselle Florence, that is an enchanting insight," I said. "From now on I shall always look at flowers in paintings and ask myself, 'Are they happy?' Many thanks."

I was feeling awkward now. Boit and I had practically fallen into a conversation, but we had not introduced ourselves. Very rude, and all my fault. The best thing to do would be to leave now. I bowed, and got control of my tongue.

"Sir, please forgive my intrusion. I wish you the best of luck with your painting. And mesdemoiselles, my thanks for your company. Good day."

"Just a moment, sir," said Mr. Boit. "Have you anything hanging here?"

Now was the time for me to say something elegant and modest about my work, smile, bow again, and lose myself in the crowd.

What came out was, "Well . . . yes—that thing over there. I did it."

Again my arm signaled the fleet.

"*Fumee d'Amber Gris*?" Boit said, reaching for me with his hand outstretched. "You are John Singer Sargent!"

It wasn't a question. If I had not been John Singer Sargent, the force of his words would have convinced me that I was.

"Sir, yes," I said, taking his hand. "I am."

"Good heavens, you're young," Boit blurted out. Then he winced at his slight rudeness. "Forgive me, please. I only meant that you're awfully young to be so accomplished."

"Well, yes," I said, blushing. "I am young, I mean."

"Girls, this is the man who did the painting that sings," Mr. Boit said.

"What song was it?" Jane asked. "What did you hear?"

"I'm afraid I didn't understand the words," I said, "so I tried to paint the music. The music is hard to describe. Very strange."

That was enough to tell the girls. There had been a hot, dark night in a city crowned with minarets. I had been making my way down an almost-deserted street, wondering if I would be attacked. Then for a moment an upstairs curtain had parted, and I had seen a beautiful woman lit by a low, golden glow. She spread her veil over her head and breathed in a rising smoke. I caught one whiff of ambergris. Beauty's fool was pierced. I had stared until the curtain dropped, knowing I would never see her again, never know who she was. My painting was my way of claiming her, keeping that moment alive. But all this was my secret.

We made our way through the crowd to my painting. The four girls studied it along with their father, Mademoiselle, and the doll. Beside me, Florence hummed "*Aprés de Ma Blonde*" very softly.

"Florence!" Mr. Boit said.

"Papa, it was P-paul," said the littlest girl. "He is a bad doll."

"Hush, Popau, or I will send you away to school with Jane," Mr. Boit replied. "Now, darlings, I am going away into this picture for a little. Don't speak again until I come back. Especially you, Popau."

Boit studied my painting as if it were an important document. His eyes went slowly back and forth, almost memorizing each stroke. And the girls let him do it in silence.

"Such light," he murmured once. "Such luminous air—"

He turned to me.

"Sir," he said. "My congratulations. I have never seen such a lustrous, subtle glow."

"Oh—Rembrandt . . . ," I said, shamelessly comparing myself to him. "Velázquez. Plenty of others."

"Perhaps, but I've never met them," Boit said. "I am deeply grateful for our encounter today."

"As am I, Mr. Boit," I said.

"Gray amber," said Jane, translating *amber gris*. "What is that exactly?"

Ambergris is sperm whale vomit, or something like it. How could I explain that?

"Uh—we get it from whales," I said. "And it smells something like sweet wood. It is used in perfumes. I suppose whales must smell very nice."

"The lady must smell nice then," Jane said.

"I'm sure of it," I said.

"I like the lady in the picture," Jane went on. "She looks very happy."

"I would like to be her," Florence agreed. "To be happy like that."

"Papa, would Mr. Sargent paint us?" Jane asked.

"Paint all of us," Mary agreed.

"Yes. Paint us happy," Florence said.

"Paint, paint," Julia added. "Paint P-paul too."

Boit broke his contemplation of my painting. He smiled.

"What about it, Mr. Sargent? Would you paint my girls? Would you give them glows like this one?"

"Paint them? Certainly I will," I said. "But I fear I'm leaving for Italy very soon. I will be gone for some time. I could begin when I come back, perhaps next winter."

"Ah," Boit said, "that will have to do then. Please look us up when you return, Mr. Sargent. We spend a great deal of time traveling. But if we are not in Paris when you get back, we will be eventually. Then we may begin at your earliest convenience."

"Please—just Sargent," I said.

I already felt very warmly toward this man who lived so happily among a bouquet of beautiful daughters. He somehow reminded me of my own dear father. Though I was living by myself now, it had not been long since I had spent long, pleasant times being taught by him.

I still went home when I wanted his advice or simply his company. Boit was clearly the same kind of man. I looked forward to the painting I would make of them. Perhaps I would cluster them together like exotic tulips in a seventeenth-century Dutch still life. With Popau as a sort of slug.

"Yes. Let's seal the bargain," he said. "Please, call me Boit."

Boit extended his hand and I took it.

"I shall. Gladly," I said.

"Very well, girls, Uncle Sargent is to paint you the next time we are all in Paris together," Boit said.

But only Julia and Mary were there to hear their father's promise. Somehow Florence and Jane had slipped away from us, and even from the hawklike gaze of Mademoiselle.

"Where have they gone now?" Boit asked no one in particular. "How did they go? Excuse us, Sargent. We must seek for the prodigal daughters. Good day."

"Good day, everyone," I said.

As we parted, I heard a couple of girlish shrieks and a babble of angry voices not far away.

"Ah," said Boit, "I believe I know where they are."

3

Iza

It was the next winter when I returned to Paris and as I had promised, looked up the Boits.

They were living in one of the splendid new apartments on the Avenue de Friedland. I had visited one or two such places before I left Paris last spring and had been most impressed with their elegance and size. That the Boits could afford such an address said they had more than enough money for anything they might want.

An exchange of notes and it was agreed that I should come there on a Tuesday afternoon in November.

It was a bitter day, with pellets of snow shooting down from the sky like buckshot. I climbed out of the dank, smelly cab, paid the driver, and climbed the steps to the Boits' door.

It was an English butler, Flint, who let me in and took my things. He was a thin, slightly gray man with glittering blue eyes. He had a rough, easy stride, and he swung his arms when he walked. In spite of his quiet and polish, he didn't seem bland enough for a butler.

I stood there alone in the foyer while he went to announce me.

The ceilings were high, the walls brightly painted with a scene of trees. It might have been beautiful in the sunlight, but the large windows behind me let in only the hopeless gray of the sky. Flanking the dark hall that led to the apartment itself were two huge matched vases. They were taller than I was, and I am more than six feet.

I was intrigued and went to examine them. They were intricately painted with Japanese designs and were lacquered to a high sheen. Even on this cloudy day they seemed to have a faint glow. They were impressive. They were meant to impress. But they were not antiques. Such things were made for the export trade. I wondered why the Boits, who could have afforded much better, put them here to welcome their guests.

I heard light, girlish feet coming toward me.

Hand in hand, Florence and Jane came to the end of the hall and stopped exactly beside one of the vases.

They were dressed as I would paint them later. Each in a black, long-sleeved frock and a schoolgirl's classroom pinafore. The dimness made their dark-stockinged legs invisible. They seemed to be floating in shadows.

Once again I was struck by their beauty. But it was a different beauty now. In the few months since I'd met them, they had changed much. I could not imagine Florence singing in public to a painting, or pointing with a dancer's foot. Jane had an edge that had not been there before. They seemed like two half-grown does stepping into a forest clearing, alert for danger. Girls must grow up to be women, and these two had started on that dark journey.

"Hello, Uncle Sargent," said Jane.

"Hello, Uncle Sargent," Florence said after her.

"Did you like Italy?" Jane asked.

"Yes. I did some good work down there, I think," I said.

Florence whispered something to Jane.

"Perhaps you should go back there, Uncle Sargent," Jane said.

Then, without speaking again, they backed up the hall and disappeared into the shadows.

Some game or other. The private world of children.

"Will you please follow me, Mr. Sargent?" Flint said, returning.

I went up the dark hall.

The parlor into which I was led was amazing. It was the richest confusion of fine furnishings and peculiar treasures. Between the paintings, the walls were hung with swords, Egyptian antiquities, Chinese dragons, even a harpoon. There were sprays of hothouse flowers sharing their vases with peacock plumes and tasseled sticks. Among the sofas and chairs were bright-patterned Turkish floor pillows and stacks of Japanese mats.

In the midst of this, carefully positioned in front of a large, white, folding screen, was a woman all in white, dressed as an Arab. An incense burner was on the floor in front of her, and she was holding a veil above her head to concentrate the smoke rising to her face.

She was an almost exact replica of *Fumee d'Amber Gris*. But the woman looked nothing like the dark, exotic creature I had painted. She was a high-colored blue-eyed blonde, and she was smiling at me.

"Welcome, Mr. Sargent," she said loudly. "Behold your creation."

"Mrs.—Mrs. Boit?" I stuttered.

"Mrs. Boit indeed," she agreed. "And your great admirer, sir."

She dropped the veil and crossed the room to shake my hand.

"I am sure my opinion of your work is even higher than Mr. Boit's, if that is possible."

I took her hand, wondering what kind of woman posed as a painting to welcome its artist. She meant it well, of course, but what sort of mind conceived such a thing?

"Thank you—very kind," I said. "Your husband—these paintings—his work?"

"Yes," she said, smiling. "My dear husband's own watercolors. I fear they are not very good, are they?"

She led me over to the harpooned wall, where three of Boit's works, all well framed, were hanging. Whatever the merits of the paintings—they were few, I confess—the merits of the man shone through them. Each pallid, flat attempt spoke of earnest attention to detail and reverence for its subject. Boit took care.

"I very much like the petals on these marigolds," I said.

Mrs. Boit laughed.

"My dear Boity has been painting for nearly fifteen years. And the best you can say is that he is rather good at marigold petals. Never mind, I cherish them all. As you can see, Mr. Sargent, I surround myself with them. I would never permit him to sell one, even if anyone wanted to buy it, for they are part of my household. And I must have my household about me wherever we travel, or I cannot be happy. And above all things, I must be happy."

It was clear to me that Mrs. Boit was—how can I put this?—her own person. I wondered if she was always so blunt.

"Your collections are indeed unique," I said.

"My collections are the story of my family," she said. "I was a

Cushing, you know. We are an old Boston seafaring family. The China trade, whaling. We have been part of it all. I come by my restlessness naturally."

She crossed the room to put herself in the brightest light and struck a pose.

"I can never be happy in one place very long," she said. "Back and forth across the Atlantic we shuttle like migrating birds. Birds who drag their nest along with them. Dear Boity is very good to put up with me."

"Indeed," I said. "I mean—"

She laughed loudly.

"I know I am not an ordinary woman, Mr. Sargent. There is no point in trying to pretend that I am."

Boit appeared in the doorway.

"Sargent, forgive me," he said. "I was—well, I was at my painting, and I simply lost track of the time. When Flint told me you were here, I was appalled at my rudeness."

"Boit, it's very good to see you again," I said, hurrying to shake his hand.

"Boity, he likes your marigold petals," Mrs. Boit said.

"Very good of him to say so."

"Just said—I mean—marigolds—difficult flower," I said.

"Perhaps more difficult for me than for you," said Boit, charming as ever. "Iza, will you ring for tea?"

So, Mrs. Boit's first name was Iza. A strange-sounding thing, and a little unpleasant. It suited her.

When the tea appeared, the three of us sat down under the one picture in the room that was not Boit's work. It was an oil portrait of

Mrs. Boit. I recognized the work of my teacher, Carolus-Duran. The small plate on the bottom of the frame read *MRS. CHARLOTTE LOUISA CUSHING BOIT*. Iza, I decided, must be a childhood name.

Carolus-Duran had painted Iza Boit sitting between the huge Japanese vases. Leaning against one was the harpoon. Her hand was slightly raised as though she were reaching for it. At her feet sat Popau, at the point of one of her shoes. Perhaps Popau was about to be kicked. It was an awkward pose. An uncomfortable picture.

"Tell me, Sargent," Boit said. "What are your thoughts on painting my girls?"

"I have had one idea," I said. "It came to me the day I met you at the Salon."

"And congratulations on your triumph there," Iza interrupted. "*Fumee d'Amber Gris* certainly merited the first prize it took."

"Thank you very much," I said. "As I meant to say, I have had a thought that your daughters are a sort of garden. I have an idea to cluster them among pots of blossoms, each of the kinds they like best. A bouquet, do you see? And, in a way, a tribute to your own interest in painting flowers, Boit."

"You understand we want something quite large," Iza said. "Something bigger than *Fumee d'Amber Gris.*"

"How large?" I said, surprised.

"Large enough to take in everything that must be there," Boit said. "It's Iza's idea that the painting will be a sort of emblem."

"It must include certain things," Iza said. "Besides myself, surrounded by my daughters, it must have Popau. And the vases."

She gestured toward her portrait. I saw her fingers curl, seeking their harpoon.

"Household gods," Boit smiled. "Our lares and penates."

Lares and penates. The household spirits of the ancient Romans, I recalled.

"Wherever we go, wherever we set up our camp, those vases mark its wall," Iza explained.

I looked at the portrait with new understanding. My teacher had painted Iza to suggest the goddess Minerva, Rome's defending spirit. The vases were her gates. The harpoon her spear. Her hair, I saw now, had been coiffed to suggest a helmet. But the doll?

"Popau must also be present, since he is the mystery at the heart of us," Iza went on. "He has been part of my family for three generations. No one recalls when he came to us or where he came from, but he was my mother's toy first. He was called Billy then. When she gave him to me, he became Horatius. Horatius was transformed into Popau by Boity when I passed him on to Florence. All the girls have played with him in turn. Now he is chiefly Julia's."

"It's an odd name," I said to Boit. "Popau. It's the pen name of that journalist who's always fighting duels here in Paris."

"Exactly," Boit said. "I have always thought Popau is a doll of bad character. A stirrer up of strife and a source of whirlwinds. The fights that Jane and Florence used to get into over him were the stuff of legend. And Mary used to blame all her misbehavior on his advice. Now Julia does so. A wicked creature, Popau."

"And my daughters are all like me," Iza Boit said. "Very much their own persons. I am sure they will all be remarkable women."

"Most men would regret having had no sons," Edward Boit said. "But I can't imagine boys being nearly as fascinating as these creatures. Trying to understand them will be a life's work."

"And they adore him for trying," Iza Boit interrupted.

"I find Florence and Jane to be a matched pair," Boit went on. "Though not a perfect match, and certainly not broken to harness yet. And Mary—"

"Mary is my little soldier," Iza Boit said. "Very loyal to me."

"And a little mother to our youngest," Boit said.

"And though she is the youngest, it's already clear that Julia will be the family beauty," Iza Boit said. "And all this must be enclosed within the frame of a portrait. So you see, Mr. Sargent, a painting of the usual size is too small. As to its price . . ." She gestured toward her husband.

Boit named a figure that made me gulp. I almost protested that it was too large. But that would have been haggling.

"Oh. Yes. Acceptable. Very," I said.

"Good," Boit said. "Though I almost wish you had said you would be too busy next year. I am leaving tomorrow for Boston. Some business back there has come up that I must deal with in person, and I expect to be away for several weeks. I very much regret that I will not be here while you are painting."

"As do I, Boit," I said. I certainly wasn't looking forward to dealing with Iza Boit alone. But having already said I wanted to start, I could hardly unsay it.

"Very well then, let the adventure begin," said Iza. "Boity, summon your darlings to the parlor."

The Adventure Begins

Julia was the first one to appear, brought by her nurse. She was hand in hand with Popau. The doll was wearing a different costume today. He was dressed as a bride. That seemed odd, knowing what I knew of him. But the child's innocent fancy delighted me.

"Do you remember Uncle Sargent, Ya-Ya?" Boit asked his daughter.

Iza for Louisa, Ya-Ya for Julia. Their nicknames were strange, as if they came from another place.

"No," said Julia, "but P-paul does."

"How do you do, Popau?" I said.

Julia put Popau's lips to her ear.

"He says, 'Go away, Uncle Sargent,'" she announced.

The adults laughed.

"Ya-Ya, you must tell Popau to be polite to Uncle Sargent," Boit said. "Uncle Sargent is here to put him in a painting. If Popau is good, he will be very famous."

Again Julia listened to Popau.

"He says 'No,'" Julia said.

Mary was next into the room. She came with a long, confident stride, like a happy boy's.

"Hello again, Uncle Sargent," she said, and sat next to Popau.

"Hello, Mary," I said.

Then we waited for the other girls to appear. The wait lengthened.

"Mary, I don't suppose your sisters are still in the schoolroom?" Boit said.

"No, Papa," Mary said. "I came at once, but they wouldn't."

"And where do you suppose they might be?" Iza asked. There was an edge to her voice.

"They ran away," Mary said.

Iza Boit forced a smile and said, "Can you not guess, darling, where they are?"

"Jane said they were going back to Boston," said Mary.

Suddenly Iza Boit leaped from her chair. She screamed at Mary, laying such a stream of words on her as I had never heard from any woman, let alone a mother speaking to her child. She raged up and down the room, waving her arms, demanding that her children be brought to her at once by the lazy, treacherous servants. It was beyond anger. It was something from the dim, dark past of humanity, when gods might seize us and shake us until we shattered. There was something ridiculous in it; Iza's white *Fumee* costume made her fury seem almost like a scene in a play, which made the reality of it more terrible.

Boit was all compassion and tenderness. He followed his wife, trying to comfort and calm her, but nothing he did was of the least help.

The girls reacted in different ways. Mary stood up, putting her hands behind her back as I had seen her do in the foyer, ready for flight or fight. Julia slid down off the sofa on which she had perched and hid under it.

I wished mightily that I had the courage to join her there.

What does one do in such a situation? I sat where I was and tried not to notice. I looked at Popau and tried to make my face as bland and dead as his.

Finally, on one of her trips around the room, Iza Boit kicked over the incense burner. Burning crumbs of sandalwood went scattering across the beautiful Samarra carpet.

At last, something I could do to help. Rather than ring for a maid, I knelt down and tried to gather up the cinders using a napkin and teaspoon.

When I did this, Mary came over and helped me.

"I think we have saved the carpet," I said, as Iza Boit slapped at her husband.

"You are a good man, Uncle Sargent," Mary said.

"Thank you," I said, feeling deeply gratified.

Then Flint was at the door with Florence and Jane. They marched before him like prisoners coming to trial. Their faces and white pinafores were blackened with soot.

"Misses Florence and Jane, sir," said Flint.

Immediately, Iza Boit's raging stopped. Or perhaps it transformed into something colder, though no less angry.

"Where have you been, children?" she asked. "We and Uncle Sargent have been waiting for you."

"In the coal bin," Jane said.

Then, as though nothing were wrong, Florence and Jane sat down. Julia came out of hiding and sat on Jane's lap. Mary followed her little sister.

"See how they have grouped themselves so naturally, Sargent?" Iza Boit asked me. "What do you think of that for an idea?"

I got control of my tongue. I would not stutter. I would not embarrass Boit further by showing my fear.

"It is a possibility," I said. "Perhaps the vases might be flanking the sofa."

"What about the light, though?" Boit said, rubbing his chin thoughtfully. "Ought it not perhaps come from that direction? I'm thinking of the shadows."

"Paint us in the cellar, then," Jane said. "It's all shadows down there."

"Don't paint anybody," Florence said.

"P-paul says, 'No,'" Julia added.

"Please don't paint us, Uncle Sargent," Mary said.

"You will be painted," Iza Boit said. "I wish it. Your father wishes it. And we will all be beautiful forever when it is done."

"When can you begin, Sargent?" Boit asked me.

More than ever I wished for some polite excuse to drop the project. I wanted no more such scenes if I could avoid them. But that was not a choice I could make. The money I would get would be shared with my parents and with my crippled sister. I was not in a position to refuse it.

I knew what my father would have told me. He would have

advised me to begin at once. "Cut straight through the torpedo line, like Farragut at Mobile Bay," he'd told me when I was growing up. "That is the best way with most unpleasant things."

"I should like to begin tomorrow," I said.

"Excellent," said Boit.

"Do you hear, children? Uncle Sargent is to paint you tomorrow," Iza Boit said.

The girls said nothing. They stared, silent as a wall, at the three of us.

"I'm glad that is settled," Iza Boit said. "Now, girls, your father has other news for you. Tell them, Boity."

"My darlings, I'm afraid I must leave you here for a little and go back to Boston alone," he said. "But at least I will not be gone for months and months this time, I promise you."

"Don't leave, we'll grieve," Florence said, and looked down at the carpet.

"Oh," said Jane. "Oh, oh. No, Papa, no."

She looked at her sister and began to murmur softly a sound that sounded like *Mumumumumum. Mumumumumum.* Perhaps it was something from babyhood, some comfort noise that they had shared. But it didn't comfort Florence now. She began to twist her hair.

Mary reached out a hand to Julia, and Julia reached out to Popau. Both younger girls began to cry.

"Darlings, I will be back before winter is over," Boit said. "Probably before Christmas."

Now all four of them were crying.

Uncomfortable as I felt, I was touched at how much the girls loved their father.

Jane lurched across the room and grabbed her father's hand.

"Papa, stay here. Don't leave us alone now," she said. She sounded desperate.

Time flows so slowly when we are young.

"I must go." Boit smiled. "But I must return too. Nothing can keep me away from my girls for very long."

"You leave, we grieve. I don't deceive," Florence said.

And Boit opened his arms to the four of them and held them tenderly while they clutched at him and wept.

"How charming they can be," said Iza Boit, sounding anything but charmed.

The cab that took me home was even damper and smellier than the one that had brought me. Outside, the darkness had wrapped itself around the city so tightly that the gas lamps barely shone above the sidewalks. Even Paris could not be beautiful on such a night.

I thought over what I had seen. Hideous as it was, I knew it was nothing so strange. I had heard of women like Iza Boit. My doctor father would have diagnosed hysteria. There was nothing to be done about hysteric women but what Boit had tried to do. Calm them if one can, ignore the event when it's over.

That was what I told myself.

I liked the girls more than ever. In spite of Jane's tongue and Florence's peculiar rhyming speech, I found them all delightful. That they could be so sweet and loving with such a mother spoke well of them and of Boit. I hoped that my portrait would convey that same quality of tenderness and truth. Be damned to Iza Boit and her cruelty and pretensions.

When I reached my apartment, I rang for tea and put on my smoking jacket. A good cigar would calm my nerves. Then I could turn my thoughts to dinner.

I puffed luxuriously and watched the smoke curl before me. Like the scent of incense.

Suddenly I laughed. *Fumee d'Amber Gris.* What kind of fool posed herself like a painting to welcome the artist? What sort of man would be impressed by such obnoxious flattery? Not John Singer Sargent.

My maid, Marianne, brought my tea. On the tray beside it was a note.

"Pardon, Monsieur Sargent," she said. "This came for you just before you returned home."

It was a bit of brown paper folded shut but not sealed. There was no stamp, no address.

"How did this come here?" I asked.

"It was shoved under the door," said Marianne. "So I assume. I found it on the floor."

"Thank you," I said.

Marianne went out, and I contemplated my evening mail.

Not only cheap brown paper, but water stained.

I opened it.

Whoever had sent it had written with a crayon. The letters were large, skewed, and ugly. The words were few.

DO
NOT
PAINT
BOITS

Demons, Demons

I stared at the paper in my hand. What could it mean? No one knew of my intention to paint the Boit girls except the Boits and myself. No one else would care. Clearly the thing was a prank; but whose prank, and why?

My cigar went out and I relit it.

Feeling rather like a detective in a story, I ran through my list of suspects. I had not sent it. That left the Boits. Edward and Iza had not done it. Boit seemed completely sincere in his desire to have me paint his family, and Iza was downright desperate. That left the girls. Julia might have written it—the letters were that crude—but why? It seemed more likely that one of the older girls had done it then, and perhaps given it to Julia to copy.

But how then had they gotten this across Paris so quickly? It had been waiting for me when I arrived home.

The answer, when it came, was so obvious that I laughed at my confusion. Clearly the girls had known that I was coming to visit. Clearly too they did not wish to be painted by me anymore. They had changed their minds since our encounter at the Salon. No doubt one of the girls had arranged in advance to have their note delivered while I was out. That level of cleverness made it certain that it was one of the two older girls. I suspected Jane but was willing to consider Florence. The first was more obviously prankish, but the second was more secretive.

What a delicious bit of childhood wickedness it was. I was more charmed than ever at the thought of spending time with my unwilling subjects. I decided I would keep the note with me when I was working at the Boits'. Perhaps I might be able to use it one day in a prank of my own.

The next day when I arrived at the Boits' home, Flint showed me into the parlor.

Iza had prepared for my coming. She was seated on a chaise longue with her daughters clustered about her. Hothouse flowers had been set about them, so many that it seemed like a jungle. The two big Japanese vases flanked the scene.

"What do you think, Sargent?" Iza Boit asked me. "Is this not the idea we want?"

"It is certainly a possibility," I said.

None of the girls was looking at me.

"Let us all turn our faces to Uncle Sargent," Iza Boit said.

It was then that Florence let me see something in her expression. It was a look that said, "Do what you will. We will do what we must."

Jane looked to her sister, then gave me a sly smile and leaned her head against Florence's knee. Then she slowly stuck out her tongue.

I choked back a laugh.

Mary automatically directed her gaze toward Iza's face.

"No, no, my dear," Iza said with an edge to her voice. "You must face Uncle Sargent."

"Yes, Mother," Mary said, and did as she was told. But one hand crept to Iza's skirt and clutched at a handful of fabric.

Satisfied that she had directed her children's gazes in the direction that suited her best, Iza Boit now gave me her profile.

I began to sketch. The first drawings were chiefly studies for mass. The relative sizes of five bodies in space, the objects around them. They were just cartoons, the faces all but featureless.

Even so, there was something about the way the girls were grouped that bothered me, though I could not have said why. Some tension was there, something was out of balance.

Then I turned to their expressions and was almost overwhelmed. There was too much in their looks: Iza Boit's domineering smile—or was it a sneer? Florence's blank, inward-turning gaze, full of sorrow, which flashed flickers of defiance. Jane's smirk hung on her lips like a scimitar, but her eyes were angry. Mary's expression was sad and solemn and steady on me—or perhaps on something behind me that only she could see. And Julia had gone into some private place with Popau and paid no attention to any of the rest of us.

I was seeing too much, feeling too much. Impressions were crowding in on me, clamoring for life on the page. The truths I was seeing were too many and too sad to be put into any portrait. No family would wish to be so exposed.

"Demons, demons," I began to mutter.

"What demons, Sargent?" Iza Boit asked.

"Oh. Forgive me," I said. "Sometimes—work comes too fast. Draws itself. Those demons."

This was true. I often experience this when I am working. But never such demons as these, or so many. Cold, sad, angry little demons were everywhere, darting among those girls and their mother.

Iza Boit laughed.

"I was sure you were referring to us."

"No—no, no," I said. "I always—often—say it. Sorry."

I came to the end of my pages.

Iza Boit stood up and held out her hand.

"May we see the first fruits?" she said.

Unwillingly, I handed over my work. What would this creature see in what I had drawn?

What she saw was exactly what she wished to see.

"When you have completed it, it will be a masterpiece," she said. "I can see it already."

"You are very kind, Mrs. Boit."

"See, girls?" Iza Boit said, showing the first sketch to her daughters. "We look just like the flowers."

Suddenly Jane snatched the sketchbook from her mother's hands and ran out of the room screaming. Florence followed her, whooping like a savage, pulling at Mary. Mary grabbed Julia's hand and dashed off after her sisters. Popau remained behind, no doubt unwillingly.

We heard their shrieks and the thunder of their feet disappearing up the hall.

Iza Boit's eyes flashed anger, but today she was able to make herself its mistress.

"Forgive us, Sargent," she said. "Just lately my children have become quite prankish."

I shrugged, making light of it.

"I only wish everyone was so anxious to possess my work," I said.

"Perhaps it would be best if you returned tomorrow," Iza Boit said. "We shall retrieve the sketches."

"Perhaps," I agreed.

Actually, that suited me perfectly. All the glamour of the Boits had fallen away for me. I had seen too much truth today for it to survive. I had seen too much to continue with my work. Reluctantly, in spite of the regret I felt over losing the commission, I knew I could never paint this picture. I needed to get away now, to spend time thinking of how I might diplomatically withdraw my services.

What we saw when we stepped out of the parlor confirmed my decision. My sketches lay scattered in scraps on the floor of the hall.

Iza Boit shrieked. She shrieked again, and Flint appeared, along with several maids.

Iza Boit stood in the middle of the hall, her head thrown back like a howling wolf, her arms rigid at her sides. She was oblivious to me, to her servants, and I believe to everything in the world except her own inhuman noise.

Flint, who had clearly seen such things often, gave orders in French.

"Take her into the master bedroom," he said. "Put a cold cloth on her face. I will come and administer the opiate in a moment."

He turned to me.

"Mr. Sargent, may I offer you your coat and hat?"

"Yes," I said.

The maids half carried, half herded Iza Boit out of sight.

One more maid, late to arrive, picked up the ruined sketches and offered them to me with a little curtsy.

When Flint had brought my coat, I stuffed the torn sketches into my pocket.

"Shall I summon a cab, sir?" Flint asked me.

"No," I said. "I prefer to walk for a while."

"Very good, sir," Flint said, and let me out of the madhouse.

Outside, the clouds were low and moved swiftly toward the south. The trees' bare branches clutched desperately at the sky as if seeking light, any light. The voice of the wind was desperate too, as desperate as Iza Boit's, but more sane. It belonged to the real world.

It was out of my way, but I turned my steps toward the Champs-Élysèes. I wanted the bustle of life around me now. There, where all the streets of Paris come together, I would be able to calm down and think.

The Champs was full of traffic, as it always was, but somehow the sounds felt muffled. Even the roar of iron tires on cobblestones was muted by the wind. I walked around and around the elegant bulk of the Arc de Triomphe and took comfort from its mighty, solid presence. I rarely gave much thought to this vast monument that the first Napoleon had built to his own egotism, but today it felt like a friend.

On my third time around, the wind began to bite deeply, and I stepped into a bistro to warm myself.

It was crowded inside, but luck was with me. A small table near the front was vacant. I ordered coffee and wine.

When I had my drinks, I took out the remains of my sketches.

Torn as they were, they looked strangely new, not merely damaged. One jagged line across Jane's face made her remaining eye not just fearful, but uncanny, as though it were looking back at me with some strange intelligence. Another had been ripped across the top, detaching Iza Boit's head. Her daughters appeared to be grouped at the foot of a ruined statue. A lower-right corner made little Julia and Popau appear to be on a desert island, or perhaps the last survivors in a drifting lifeboat, without hope of rescue.

Without hope of rescue. I had caught something there. Perhaps all the girls felt need of rescue. Certainly I could see their point. But it was not my place to interfere. And, I reminded myself, all I really wanted to do was to extricate myself from the situation.

I turned one of the torn bits of paper in my fingers. It was the part with Iza Boit's head. Held upside down, I saw something strange in it, something I had not even known I was drawing.

It is difficult to describe, for it was not there in any visible way. And how does an artist draw what he doesn't see? Nonetheless, there was something in the shadows behind Iza Boit's head. Something I had suggested in the way I drew the shadows, shadows that had not been there in reality. Shadows I had added only for contrast.

I looked at all the scraps. In each one, wherever there was a bit of background, I saw the thing that wasn't there. I could not say what it was, only that it was there; and I had drawn it without consciously seeing it.

I was certain it was evil. There was something sinister in it. A leer without a face, and a sense of fangs behind the leer. A gleaming, greedy squint loomed over the girls. Nothing physical was there; but in the smudges I had made, a hideous thing was lurking.

"Well, Sargent," I told myself. "You are the sensitive one. Overwhelmed by your own feelings, and drawing spooks in the corners."

I began to fold the papers in fours to dispose of them more easily. Last of all, I quartered the one with Iza Boit's head.

Written on the back, scratched into the paper, were two words that must have been scrawled with a fingernail. If I had held the paper away from the light, I would never have seen them.

HELP US

My first thought was that this was another prank, like DO NOT PAINT BOITS. But no. This had not been planned. One of the four of them had done this swiftly, in the hope that I would see it somehow. She had wanted it to be secret. A secret from whom? Iza? One of her sisters? Something else, lurking in the shadows? Was I the only one who sensed demons in the dark?

I studied each of the scraps again, looking for clues in the beautiful faces. Which of these girls was afraid, and of what was she afraid?

It was impossible to say which girl had written the words. And it was impossible for me to ignore them. However much I might wish to do so, I could not give up the painting now. Be damned to the painting itself, be damned to the laws of polite society. This was a call for help, and it had touched me to the heart.

My father, I knew, would have turned aside to offer his services to a stranger in a medical emergency; I had seen him do it. And what man, finding a note washed up on the beach in a bottle, would not try a rescue? There might be nothing I could do. Probably this was so. But if there was even a small chance that I could save the Boits from the lurking menace in their shadows, I must chance it. And then, like sunrise inside me, I thought of how I might begin.

6

In The Schoolroom

An exchange of notes later that day settled that I would come again on the following morning, an hour later than before.

When Flint let me in, I saw that the big Japanese vases were back in the foyer. I wondered what scene Iza Boit had prepared for me to view today.

As it turned out, she was perfectly normal when I was shown in to her. Indeed, she looked more normal than I had ever seen her. I supposed that was her latest performance.

"Good morning, Sargent," she said.

"Good morning, Mrs. Boit," I replied.

She indicated that I might sit down, and I took a chair beside her.

"What do you think of our work so far?" Iza Boit said.

It was the perfect opening for me to begin the plan that had come to me yesterday in the bistro.

"I think there are tensions," I said. "Artistic tensions, that is. I am not sure that I see how to resolve them."

"Artistic tensions of what sort?" Iza Boit said.

"Well, perhaps you can help me," I said. "I am not quite sure what they are. Perhaps you have some feelings on the matter."

She smiled. Then she closed her eyes in thought. Then she smiled again. My flattery was working, so far.

"All I can say is that you are right," she said. "There are tensions, problems with the entire concept."

"Concept, yes, thank you," I said. "I think I have it now. It seems to me to be a question of mass. Five of you. Six with Popau. All different sizes. And the vases. It makes for crowding."

"Crowding, yes, exactly!" Iza Boit said, leaning in toward me. "I felt it keenly yesterday but could not name the feeling."

"There is another thing, I think," I said. "If I were to describe you as music, I should say you were a full chord. Your daughters are still single notes. And each note is different, and they do not all complement one another or the chord."

Iza Boit laughed with pleasure. I was pleased as well. I had practiced that speech.

"Then what are the vases, Sargent?" she said. "What part of music are they?"

"The vases? Oh—the pedals on the piano, I suppose."

It was the first thing that came into my head, but Iza Boit laughed again.

"Boity has done well to bring you among us," she said. "Such insight you have, Sargent. You must find a way to proceed."

"I fear I don't quite see how," I said.

"Surely there must be some way," Iza Boit said. "Boit wishes you to paint our daughters. I desire it."

Iza Boit's eyes flickered with delight. Then she said exactly what I had been hoping to lead her to say.

"Perhaps you should paint us separately," she said. "I in one portrait, the girls in another."

I pretended to hesitate.

"Yes, that could be the solution," I said. "But which one first?"

I watched her features work as she turned the idea over in her mind. She wanted to be painted now, right away; I could see that. But she wanted even more for me to see her as a person putting art above all.

"You should begin with the girls, I think," she said.

"Then I shall," I said.

"I will have Flint show you to their schoolroom," Iza Boit said. "They should be there in a few moments for their morning lessons. Spend an hour with them and see what may come to you. This time, sir, guard your sketchbook."

The schoolroom was on the second floor. It was a large and airy place, equipped with everything a governess or tutor might want. A large blackboard had been hung on the wall, and on this was written a poem in colored chalk. Against the wall opposite was a small harmonium with shining ivory keys. There were portraits of Washington, Lincoln, and Napoleon, a bust of Shakespeare, and a French-English dictionary on a stand. Besides these, there was a large globe in one corner. I gave it a spin and was pleased to see that it was modern enough to show Colorado, the newest state.

The sound of feet behind me made me turn.

"Hello, Jane." I smiled.

Jane did not answer. She moved across the floor to the window in three long glissades, like a ballerina.

"Did you hear me coming?" she asked.

"Yes," I said.

"Liar," she said. "You only heard me at the last second, when I came in. I was following you all the way from the salon. You didn't know."

"You're quite right," I said.

"I'm a very good sneak," Jane said. "Even better than Florence. I can sneak anywhere."

"That's a very useful talent," I said.

"Very, very useful," Jane agreed. "I learn lots of things from sneaking."

She stood *en pointe* and raised her arms over her head.

"Did you come to make more sketches for me to rip up?" she said.

"I came to make more sketches," I said.

"Well, you'll have to wait," she said. "The other three are hiding."

"Why aren't you hiding?" I said.

"Because I'm not afraid of you," she said.

"That's good," I said. "There's no reason to be."

"You don't know that," Jane said. "You don't know everything there is to be afraid of."

"That's true," I said. "There must be something to be afraid of that I haven't met yet."

"Maybe you should be afraid of me, Uncle Sargent," she said.

I laughed.

"I could kill people and get away with it," Jane said. "I could sneak up behind them and just do it. Did you ever kill anyone, Uncle Sargent?"

"No," I said. "Anyway, not yet. Have you?"

"I'm not telling," Jane said.

"That isn't fair," I said. "I told you."

"But how do I know you were telling me the truth?" Jane said, and began to prance around the room in *relevès*.

"I always tell the truth," I said.

"Well, I don't," Jane said.

"Is that the truth?" I asked.

"Yes—no—I mean—" and the girl laughed hard and long. Then she said, "Suppose I promised always to tell you the truth. Would you believe me?"

"I promise," I said.

"But what if I lie?" she said.

"Then I will be fooled," I said. "But what good will that do you?" Jane considered this.

"Then I won't lie if you won't lie," she said. "Promise?"

"Certainly. Look that way," I said.

With her face in profile, Jane said, "What do you think of Mother?"

"A gentleman couldn't possibly answer that question," I said, whipping my pencil across the paper. "And a young lady shouldn't ask it."

"Why not?"

"Because some things are private," I said.

"Some things are very, very private," Jane said. "Those are the ones worth knowing."

I went on sketching her.

"I'll tell you something very, very private," she said. "Papa is the best husband in the world, but Mother doesn't like him much."

I could feel myself blushing. I looked down at my sketch to try to hide it.

"You dance very well," I said.

"Uncle Sargent, are you married?" Jane asked, ignoring my compliment.

"No," I said.

"Why not?"

"That's one of those very private things," I said.

"I just told you one," Jane said.

"But I didn't ask—Oh, very well, Jane," I snapped. "I will tell you a truth and then we will stop this."

I took a deep breath and said, "I was engaged about a year ago. I was in love. But then I painted the young woman, and I found I wasn't in love anymore. All the love had gone into the painting."

Why would a man say something like that to a child? But Jane had got me off balance.

"That is the truth," Jane said, looking at me hard. "You did tell me the truth." Then she grinned and shouted, "You told me the truth, you told me the truth! And I lied to you! Ha-ha, I lied! Good-bye, Uncle Sargent."

And she ran out of the room.

I stood there, furious and idiotic.

"Damn!" I whispered over and over again. "Damn, damn, damn, damn, damn."

Someday, I promised myself, I would be done with portraits and only paint flowers, like Boit. Flowers are what they are.

Some minutes passed, and I calmed down a little.

At last the Boit girls appeared in the doorway, all four of them.

"He's here again," Florence murmured.

"It's nice to see you again, Uncle Sargent," Jane said, and once more stuck out her tongue.

Mary and Julia were accompanied by a delicate-looking young woman no larger than Jane, and, as always, by Popau.

"Hello, Uncle Sargent," Mary chirped.

"Uncle Sargent, Popau still says 'No.'" Julia told me.

"This is Miss Joseph," Jane said. "She is going to die horribly."

"Horribly," said Julia.

"Stone dead," Florence agreed.

Miss Joseph seemed to be used to being told that she was about to be murdered. At any rate, she showed no surprise.

"Sir," said the young woman.

"Permit me," I said. "I am John Singer Sargent. I have been engaged to paint the children."

"I was not informed of your coming," Miss Joseph said.

"I believe Mrs. Boit had the idea to send me here only this morning," I said.

"I see," said Miss Joseph. "Well, how do you wish to proceed?"

"He mustn't," Florence said.

"He won't," Jane said.

One of these girls has called for help like a drowning sailor, I reminded myself. Which one? I studied them, looking for clues. It was impossible to say. But I noticed Florence's eyes on my sketch pad as if it were a weapon pointed at her.

"Tell me, girls," I said, "what would you think if I were to paint only you, without your mother. Would that be a good idea?"

Florence and Jane looked at each other.

"He's not going to leave," Jane said quietly to her sister.

Florence closed her eyes. She began to sway gracefully back and forth with her arms over her head. She stamped her feet. It looked a little like a flamenco danced by someone who had never seen one.

"Florence, my dear, are you well?" Miss Joseph asked.

We all stood looking at Florence for what seemed like a very long time.

"Dare the gate, meet your fate," was all she said when she finally spoke.

"Dare the gate, meet your fate," she repeated.

It was an incantation, I thought. A charm of some kind.

Now all eyes turned toward me. On the faces of the two older girls, I saw the wariness. On Mary's face the grave, brave look of a guardian angel as she clutched Julia's hand. Julia's expression was as blank and unreadable as Popau's. And in Miss Joseph's eyes was a mute cry of fear.

I wanted to break this mood, whatever it was. I sat down at the harmonium, ran my fingers over the keys, and began. I did not look at the girls or speak. I simply played the little melody every child in France knows, about dancing around and around on the broken bridge of Avignon. As I played, I made each repetition a little more elaborate, a bit more fantastic. I let out the anger I felt, let it pass into the music.

After a few moments, I heard Mary's voice,

"Sur le Pont d'Avignon
L'on y danse, l'on y danse,
Sur le Pont d'Avignon
L'on y danse tout en rond."

Florence began to dance. Jane joined her. Mary danced with Julia and Popau.

I went on playing, verse after verse, while the girls flung themselves about more and more freely Miss Joseph stood with her back against the wall and smiled.

At last, they formed a chain, with Jane at the head, Florence behind her, then Mary, Julia and Popau. In and out among the desks they wove until they were flushed and smiling, all but the doll.

I played a last crashing chord and bellowed,

"l'on y danse
Tout en round!"

Across all barriers of age and experience, for a moment we were friends.

Florence whispered something to Jane.

Jane said, "If we let you paint us, how will you do it? Will you make us look like flowers? We don't want that. We hate all flowers but Papa's."

"I was thinking I might portray you as Indians in front of a burning cabin," I said.

Jane and Mary laughed. Florence smiled sadly.

"Or if that doesn't suit you, what about something like *The Janus*

Gate? The four of you lurking in the shadows, ready to set upon those old women and rob them."

A little more laughter.

Florence whispered to Jane again.

"Paint us like the Arab lady," Jane said. "We dare you."

"The woman in *Fumee d'Amber Gris*?" I asked.

"Yes," Jane said.

"Your parents will never approve of it," I said. "What about this? I will paint you as you are dressed now, but I will paint you in the style of Velázquez, the great Spanish artist. I know your father would like that. He admires Velázquez's work."

Florence looked down. Then, after a long moment, she said, "Play the music in the lady's picture."

"It was something like this," I said, and began to play a simple tune I'd heard on the street in Tunis. It was not a true Arab song but sounded vaguely like it.

Once again Florence began to sway, raising her arms and lowering them, stamping her feet erratically.

Jane clapped her hands, trying to keep time and failing. Mary and Julia skipped around their sisters in a circle.

They were trying to create the dance of the perfume from what they had seen in my painting. What rich, elaborate imaginations they had. I was charmed again in spite of the sadness I felt lay at the heart of their dance.

Miss Joseph, I noted, was biting her lip and fluttering her fine-boned hands. The strangeness of what her students were doing was quite beyond her.

Then, in the middle of the third or fourth repetition of the song,

Florence suddenly stopped moving and sat down at her desk.

The other girls stopped when she did and took seats, all but Julia, who went to a corner with Popau.

"Our time is nearly up," I said. "I'll just do one or two sketches of each of you."

Quickly, I did a few drawings. Then I tore them out of my book and handed them to each of the girls.

"I don't ever want you to feel frightened or worried about being drawn or painted," I said. "It should be a friendly thing between us."

Florence took her drawings, stared at them, and let them fall to the floor.

Jane took a pen and drew mustaches on her pictures.

"I always wondered how I'd look with whiskers," she said. "See, Uncle Sargent? You should paint me like this."

No one else spoke.

I walked over and added a Van Dyke beard to the mustache.

"Even better," I said. "This brings out your noble profile."

Jane laughed, then looked at Florence and stopped.

I flourished a drawing I had made of Miss Joseph and gave it to her.

"Thank you for indulging me this morning, Miss Joseph," I said. "It is much appreciated."

Miss Joseph looked at the sketch.

"Sir, you flatter me, I fear," she said.

She blushed, and that made her delicate little face quite beautiful for a moment.

It made me long to say something gallant, such as, "Flattery is quite unnecessary, I assure you." But that might be too bold. What came out instead was, "Oh, no. Rough thing. Cartoon, really."

Miss Joseph blushed again, and I looked away in embarrassment. My eyes fell on Florence and Jane, who were looking at us over the tops of Jane's sketches.

"Monsters lurk in your work," Florence said. "Lay them bare if you dare."

"Yes," Jane said. "If you dare. We don't care."

She gave her scimitar smile again.

I had no idea what any of that meant. Nor did I yet have the least clue which of these girls had cried for help. But it seemed that they would agree to being painted. That was as much progress as I could make in one day.

To my surprise, Miss Joseph accompanied me as I left the room.

"Are you determined to paint the Boits, sir?" she whispered to me.

"Painting is how I earn my living," I said.

"Then, sir, let me tell you one thing that may help you. Believe nothing that you hear in this house. Believe less than half of what you see. Good day."

And Miss Joseph was gone.

A Visit Home

That night I went across town to see my family.

When the maid let me in, my sister, Emily, jumped up and ran across the room to kiss me. I put my arms around her and wished for the hundred millionth time that it had been I and not she who had been crippled with a bent spine. I would still have had my talent for painting. Emily's great gift was for loving, but what man would ever know it?

"Johnny, Johnny," she said, as I carefully hugged her. "You should have come for dinner."

"I really came for a cigar with Father," I said. And out of my coat I took a few well-wrapped Havanas and held them out to him.

"And perhaps a glass of port," my father said, straightening his long, spidery body to greet me.

"I would like that very much," I said.

"Why didn't you bring a friend?" Mother said.

"It was a sudden decision to come tonight," I said. "I'll bring someone next time, Mother, I promise."

What Mother meant was "Why didn't you bring an artist or painter whom I can chatter with?" Mother gets great pleasure from talking to artists. The pleasure is, unfortunately, rather onesided.

"Well," said my father. "The port is in my study. Come, John."

"Don't stay in there all night, Fitzwilliam," Mother called after us.

"I am going to smoke with my son, John," he replied.

I warmed at the note of pleasure in his voice.

My father, Fitzwilliam Sargent, might have been one of the greatest doctors in America. But then I would never have been born.

If he had married someone other than my mother, he would certainly have stayed at home in Philadelphia. He would have taken care of his patients there, in the city he loved, and done some research. I really think he might have discovered something wonderful. And whatever boy came into the light instead of me would have grown up there, among his cousins, aunts, and uncles, and known the same stones and street corners as Ben Franklin. If that boy had been anything like me, he would have been happy. Who can say whether he would have become an artist or not?

Instead, my father had married my mother. She was a Philadelphian as well, but America held no charms for her. She wanted art, history, and literature. She wanted Europe.

There was nothing wrong with any of that. But once she and Father were there, she became unwell every time he wanted to return to our own country. For some reason, she never became ill traveling from France to England to Italy to Germany, or wherever she wanted to go next. It was only the prospect of seeing America again that seemed to affect her health.

So they stayed, and both we children were born here. By birth I am an Italian. My sister is French. But we feel as American as the Adirondacks or the Susquehanna River.

We were never rich. Father had a small inheritance, and Mother's was somewhat larger. No doubt we were very much better off than most people. But in order to exist as Mother wished us to do, we had to live in the unfashionable places of Europe, or visit the fashionable ones in the unfashionable seasons. This, I think, would have been all right with me if we could have stayed in one place. I could have given my heart to Brittany or to Florence, if I could have grown up there.

Instead, I learned to love beauty detached from any place. Perhaps in that I am lucky.

Perhaps.

My father's study was about the size of a generous closet. With a rolltop desk, two worn easy chairs, and a bookcase filling almost every inch, there was barely room for two men to move; but I loved this small, quiet place where the two of us could be together.

Father was very ceremonious with our cigars. He took out a pair of tongs to hold his and cut the tips of both of our smokes with a little brass clipper. The remaining four cigars he put into the mahogany humidor I'd given him some years ago.

Our port, along with two glasses, he took from a cheap glass decanter he kept on the bookcase.

One day soon, I promised myself, I would buy him something better for his wine.

We lit, and the rich smoke wove between us like the visible bonds of our love. My father smiled. It was something he rarely did.

"Excellent," he said, blowing a ring of smoke toward the ceiling. "Shakespeare, I think."

This was one of his jokes. Cigar makers hire readers to entertain them while they are rolling cigars all day long. In some factories the workers want to hear cheap fiction and magazine articles, while in others they listen all day to the classics. Father claimed that he could tell what the cigar makers had been listening to by the quality of the smoke.

I puffed again.

"*Macbeth*," I said.

"*Macbeth*," my father said. "Assassinations. Witches. An ambitious woman. Which of them have you come to see me about?"

"How did you know I was here to consult?" I asked.

"You come on a Friday, which you rarely do. You bring no friend for your mother, which means you do not want to spend time with her tonight. You bring me a present of excellent tobacco, which is an excuse for men to go off by themselves. So I flatter myself that you want to see me about something important. Then you mention *Macbeth*, not, let us say, *The Comedy of Errors*. So I guessed one of the three subjects I mentioned might be on your mind. Am I right?"

"I've come to the right man," I said. "But I can't say which of the subjects you've mentioned is the one I'm here to ask about. Perhaps witches is the closest."

"Take a look at these," I said, holding out some of my torn sketches of the Boits. "Tell me what you see. Don't neglect the backgrounds."

I have always thought of my father as a man of one color, a rich gray. It is the gray that underlies all my portraits. Sometimes, when he was teaching me and Emily our lessons, he would become a very handsome blue; and I have seen flashes of black in him when he speaks of my sister's crippled back, or of the Confederacy. But now, as he examined the sketches from every angle, I saw an electric yellow flashing in him more and more strongly.

"Are these childen really as unhappy as you've made them?" he asked me finally.

"I think they are," I said.

"Tell me about them," Father said.

I told him about my first meeting with Boit and his daughters. I told him everything that I had seen at the apartment on the Avenue de Friedland.

When I was finished, he said, "I can certainly see why you feel yourself one with them."

"They're only little girls, Father," I said. "What can we have in common?"

"A great deal," Father said. "First of all, these children wander over the world, as you have done. Quite likely, they feel connected to no place. They must have no friends but one another. That was often your case, yours and Emily's. Also, they have a mother who is determined to see herself as a creature who is outside the common herd. So have you. Small wonder you like them so well, or feel their sorrow so strongly. You might almost be part of the same family."

"There is more," I said. And I told him the strange things: The note warning me not to take the commission, the words scratched in the torn-up sketch.

"And although you haven't seen them," I said, "I keep finding strange things in the shadows of the sketches. Never when I'm draw-ing. Only later when I look at them again."

"You mean these things in the background are there by accident?" my father said.

He put down his cigar and picked up the sketches again.

"I thought they were some kind of artist's joke," he said. "Not your usual sense of humor, Johnny, but these are not usual people. No, I suspect they are highly unusual, and fated to become more so."

"What do you mean?" I asked.

"I see the beginnings of madness in two of these faces," he said. "The older ones. They are not the faces of innocent children. They have looked into some well of bitterness. What they have seen down there is what you are drawing, I think."

"How can I be drawing something inside of them?" I asked.

"Isn't that your trade?" Father asked. "Drawing what's inside people?"

"But they're so young," I said. "Isn't madness usually something that comes late in life? Or even at birth? But not now, when they're just—well, when they're just becoming women."

"It's more common than you'd think," Father said. "And from what you tell me of Mrs. Boit, it may be in their blood. That is the usual explanation. Or perhaps they are simply finding the burden of their mother's peculiarities more than they can carry."

I took a deep breath.

"I'm not sure that what I'm drawing is inside them, sir," I said.

"Hm," Father said, "that brings us back to witches. Or perhaps to ghosts."

"You don't believe in such things," I said. "Neither do I."

"No, we don't," Father said. "We're the sensible Sargents. And yet—isn't a portrait a kind of ghost? A trace of someone that lingers after they are gone? Not the person himself, of course. Nothing alive in it. But the semblance of life. The memory of something that was there. And what else is a spirit supposed to be?"

"I don't follow you," I said. "What are you suggesting?"

"What is art?" Father said. "We don't know. All we know is, only human beings make it. And perhaps, besides all the ways that there are to make art, there may be other ways that we do not know. Art we make when we are not even trying, using materials—better to call them forces perhaps—which we are unaware of. Perhaps what you are sensing is along those lines."

"What do you think I should do?" I asked.

"What do you want to do?" Father asked me.

"I want to help those children, if I can," I said.

"Ah," Father said. His cigar glowed and faded while he thought over what to say next. At last he said, "There is another way in which you resemble these girls, John. Please, don't be hurt when I tell you this. But you are only a little more mature than they are."

I laughed.

"I can assure you, Father, I'm not angry," I said. "But what a thing to say."

But my father didn't even smile.

"You didn't have much of a boyhood, Johnny," he said. "All you ever really had was art. Art and your piano. You had me, your mother, and your sister, of course. But you never had a single boy with whom you could chum around, wasting time. You never had a friend your own age, or even the chance of making one. That leaves a hole."

His cigar went out and he relit it.

"You know I always wanted you to join the navy," he said. "You could so easily have gotten into the academy and become an officer. That would have given you something of what you missed, I think. The companionship of good fellows."

"I'm very happy to be what I am," I said.

"It's a fine life." My Father nodded. "But not an adventurous one. And now, I think, you sense an adventure. The sort of spook story every boy loves to hear about. And it's real. Something very strange is happening to these girls. And you want to be part of it, just as any boy would."

"Father, really—" I began.

But he held up his hand.

"I know you meant every word about wanting to help," he said. "But there is always more going on in us than we say. And it is the unspoken things that are the strongest."

"If that is true, then I thank you for telling me," I said. "It may be very helpful. But it doesn't change anything."

My father sighed heavily.

"Then, my brave son, go and try. But remember that you are dealing with dangerous things. The Boits are strange. If there is a scandal involving this painting, that will be very bad for your career. And there may be worse dangers than that. Things unimaginable. Be careful."

8

"She's Calling, She's Calling"

I spent the next several days sketching the girls. Each morning, Flint led me to a different room, Miss Joseph fetched the children to it, and I started making pictures.

I might have stopped at any time and said, "Girls, which one of you wrote 'Help us'? I want to help you. Of what help can I be?"

But I held back. Whichever one of them it was, she was afraid to speak in front of the others; and none of them ever saw me alone, as Jane had that day in the schoolroom.

I feared too that something lurking nearby might hear me and be warned.

I saw it most often in the pictures of Florence and Jane. Then it was almost another person, smirking or leering above them. When I drew Mary, the thing seemed to be in profile, if it came at all. With Julia it was smaller but thicker than with the others. Sometimes I even found it clinging to Popau.

Did the girls know it was there? They must feel something. Wasn't this the thing from which at least one of them wanted to be rescued?

They gave no sign of it. When they were with me, they ignored me almost completely. When they came into whatever room Flint had taken me, Florence always dropped me a deep, sarcastic curtsy. Jane bowed and stuck out her tongue. Mary said, "Good morning, Uncle Sargent," and Julia simply looked at me, then whispered something to Popau.

Then they wandered around whatever room we were in, shouting, bickering, and playing. I might have been as inhuman as Popau as far as they were concerned.

Each day Iza Boit examined my sketches. Each day she approved my work but shook her head over the rooms.

"We must try, try again," she said.

Toward the end of the week, I was beginning to think that Jane's suggestion of the coal bin might be the right one after all. We had tried the schoolroom again, the salon again, the small salon, and the dining room. Today we were in the music room.

"Today, Uncle Sargent, we will delight you with our new tone poem, 'Siegfried the German goes Mad,'" Jane announced.

She and Florence sat down at the piano.

"I sometimes enjoy music when I work," I said.

"Well, you won't enjoy this," said Jane.

They started smashing the keys, playing two different songs.

"We changed our minds. It's not a tone poem, it's an opera," Jane shouted.

She began to sing,

"Siegfried the German
Tried to paint, tried to paint, tried to paint.

A lady came and made him faint,
My fair lady."

Mary joined in. Julia accompanied her sisters, singing, "Ya-Ya,Ya-Ya,Ya-Ya, Ya-Ya," and banging on a drum made from a footstool.

I studied the room.

I didn't like the light there. In summer it would have been in full glare, but in winter it was dim. Not shadowy, but gray. I wanted more light, to create some true shadows.

I sent for Flint.

"Flint, would it be possible to have that large mirror in the hall brought into this room and set there, where it will reflect what light we have?" I asked. I had to speak almost directly into his ear to be heard.

"Of course, sir," Flint said.

In a quarter of an hour, he and a footman were back with the mirror, a huge and heavy thing in a dark frame.

When it came into the room, the concert stopped.

"P-paul says no," Julia said, and ran to her doll.

"Flint, you must put that back at once," Florence commanded. "Back at once, you dunce!"

Ignoring her perfectly, Flint and his helper went out of the room.

"Flint, come back here!" Jane shrieked.

In the reflection I saw Florence and Jane standing up behind the piano. Mary had crossed to Julia and taken her hand. Each of their faces was riveted on the mirror in fear.

It was now or never, I decided. Let whatever was listening hear what I said next. My father's old advice came back to me: "Go straight through the torpedo line, like Farragut at Mobile Bay."

I turned to them.

"Girls, which one of you asked me for help? I want to help. Tell me what I need to do."

Now the three oldest ones looked at one another.

"It wasn't me," said Mary.

"Yes, it was, you little sneak," Jane hissed.

She slapped her sister.

Screaming, Mary ran out of the room, dragging Julia.

Popau fell from Julia's grip and lay on the floor by the footstool.

"Please, Uncle Sargent, put it back," Florence implored me.

"Florence, what's wrong?" I said. "It's just a mirror. It's here to light up one side of the room a little better, that's all. What are you afraid of?"

She didn't answer.

"Look," Jane whispered.

I turned back to the mirror.

In one corner of it, a pale light began to gleam. It was not a reflection. It was coming from within the mirror, or behind it. Pale, indefinite, wavering, it grew from a nebulous patch the size of my fist to something larger than my head. It flashed brilliantly, and faded.

"It didn't happen," Jane said.

"What?" I demanded. "What didn't happen?"

I crossed the room to the piano and clumsily wedged myself in behind it.

"None of it happened," Jane said.

"Jane, tell me," I said. "I need to know what you know. I see what you see in the shadows, but I don't know what it is. Help me."

"No one can help you," Florence said. "It's too late."

"Too late for what?" I said.

Then clearly, from above and behind me, I smelled burning ambergris.

Just one whiff, sharp and real as if I were in a lady's bedroom. Intimate, arousing, and impossible. Impossible as what I had just seen in the mirror.

"She's calling, she's calling," Florence said with wild joy.

She pushed me away with a strength I would never have guessed she had and grabbed Jane. Out of the room they ran, and down the hall.

I hesitated, then went after them, calling, "Jane, Florence, come back. Don't run from this thing. Come back and face it."

When I reached the doorway, the hall was empty. There was no sound of their feet.

They must be somewhere close by, but it would be unforgivably rude of me to go from room to room, searching for them. I couldn't go ranging through the Boits' home. The girls might as well have dropped off the face of the earth.

I turned back to the mirror. It was normal now. All I saw were my own face, stupid with surprise, and the room behind me.

The perfume lingered, teasing me. It was as if the thing that had made the light in the mirror knew that. As if it was scorning me. I felt embarassed, threatened.

"What is it?" I asked the empty room. "What are you?"

It was only when the odor was gone that I saw what wasn't in the mirror any longer.

Popau was gone.

I had seen Julia drop that damned doll. I'd heard its china head hit the carpet. It had been lying by the footstool.

Hadn't it?

I looked under every piece of furniture in the room. I searched behind the curtains. It wasn't the doll I wanted, it was the rationality that told me it was there. I wanted that badly.

I almost called out its name, but the words caught in my throat.

She's calling, she's calling.

What had that meant? Whatever Florence's words signified, whether some clue to this madness I was in or madness itself, one thing was clear. I was no longer watching some children's game. This was something real.

"Or perhaps not real but definitely serious," I muttered, rubbing my chin. Then, "Good grief, Sargent, what the devil do you mean by that?"

Then Flint was there.

"I beg your pardon, sir. Have you any further need of the mirror?" he asked.

"No, I guess not," I said. "Take it back, Flint."

"Very good, sir."

"Flint do you smell anything?" I blurted out.

"Sir?" Flint said.

"Never mind. Sorry," I said.

Then I had a thought. There was one person here who might be able to help me now.

"Flint, would Miss Joseph be in the schoolroom?"

"I believe so, sir," Flint said.

"Thank you. I may just put my head in there before I go," I said.

"Very good, sir," Flint said. "I'll get help to replace the mirror."

I went down the hall to the schoolroom.

Miss Joseph wasn't there, but Mary and Julia were, hiding under Mary's desk.

"Mary, darling, are you all right?" I asked.

I knelt down beside the girls and put my hand on Mary's trembling shoulders.

"Go away, Uncle Sargent, I want my mother," she sobbed.

"I'll send for her as soon as someone comes," I said. "I'm afraid I don't know where she is."

"Uncle Sargent, you made it come," Julia said.

"Why did you do that?" Mary said.

"Do what, Mary?" I asked. "What did I make come?"

"We want Mother!" Mary shouted.

She jerked out from under the desk and ran away, with Julia behind her.

It wasn't long before they were back, with Miss Joseph shepherding them.

"Miss Joseph, I'm afraid something very . . . very odd has happened," I said.

I saw the fear in her eyes that had been there before, the day the girls danced.

"What have you seen?" she said.

Clearly there was more in my own face than I had realized.

"I don't know," I replied. Then I asked, "Did Florence and Jane come this way?"

It was a stupid question, and I knew it.

"Wherever they are sir, they are far from you and me," Miss Joseph said.

Then she turned to Mary and Julia, who were still howling for their mother.

"There, my dears, there, there," she kept saying. "It's all right now. Your mother made it all right. She wants you to be happy, darlings. She wants you to go to the nursery. Come on now, won't that be nice? Mary, be a brave little soldier. We'll play house."

Ignoring me, she dragged and pushed the sobbing girls away.

Clearly it was time for me to go. I wondered if I would ever be asked back to coninue my work.

Down the hall, down the stairs I went.

I wondered where Iza Boit was. Out visiting? It was that time of day. Or was she lying in a dark room with a cold cloth on her face and a dose of opium in her veins? Or was she simply sitting somewhere in the beautiful modern apartment oblivious to everything going on beyond her door?

Flint was waiting in the foyer. He had been expecting me.

The mirror was already back in its place.

"Flint, did you see where the Misses Boit went?" I asked.

"No, sir," he said.

"They ran out of the room, you know," I said. "They seemed

quite badly frightened by something. I'm worried that they may have gone out unaccompanied. Are you sure that none of them ran out the door?"

"I believe not, sir, " Flint said.

"Do you have any idea where they did go?"

"No, sir," said Flint. "The comings and goings of the children are the concern of Miss Joseph."

"And yet you did know to search for Miss Florence and Miss Jane in the coal bin that first day I came."

"It was not the first time they had hidden there, sir," Flint said. "May I help you with your coat?"

A moment later I was out on the street.

Las Meninas

I walked a long time through the dark streets of Paris that night.

Help us. Help us. Those words were before my eyes like black flames. They were all I had to cling to.

I am a man who likes to feel the ground under his feet. Or I want to be lifted off them by some moment of transcendent beauty. I do not want to feel myself falling into some maelstrom of darkness.

Florence. Jane. Mary. Julia. Miss Joseph. Flint. Iza. And Boit himself. What mysteries were they hiding? And from whom? Outsiders? Each other? Themselves?

I had allowed myself to be drawn in, and now I was without an idea of what was going on, or a clue about what to do next.

When I finally returned home, my feet tired and my shoes soaked through, I found the usual note from Iza Boit, setting an appointment for the next day.

I crumpled it up and threw it in the fire.

The next day. Tomorrow it would be expected that I should begin the preliminary work on the canvas. I must do it, but how?

What was I to show to the world about the Boits?

"Solid black," I said to the fire. "And across the top the words 'Ask No Questions And You Will Be Told No Lies.'"

I turned the tortured faces in that place on the Avenue de Friedland over and over in my mind, as I had the torn sketches that day in the bistro. Who, if anyone, was telling me the truth?

Iza Boit? The truth, whatever it might be, was not in that poor, mad, angry woman. She was bitterly struggling to create a world she could control. Anything of which she could not be mistress would be kept outside her gates.

The girls? They were deep into some secret, but what did they really know about it? I was sure they were reacting to something coming at them out of the dark. Most probably they did not know the truth.

Then there was Flint. Whatever he knew would stay locked behind his lips. That would be true of any decent butler. Know everything, say nothing. From what I had seen for myself, he was only a man who was doing his job. A difficult job, and he seemed to do it well.

Boit? I suspected that Boit, with his sunny nature, knew nothing whatever of what had come upon his family. He loved his wife and daughters and saw them through the lens of his love. Besides, he was far away. If he was often apart from them, he might be nothing but a charming visitor to his own home.

That left Miss Joseph. Miss Joseph had told me—what? That she was frightened. That she did not understand what was going on around her. Nothing in her life would have prepared her to educate such girls. She must have joined the household imagining pleasant hours in the schoolroom teaching French and history to playful, curious, loving children. Or was she the innocent she seemed? Was she as frightened as I took her to be? Perhaps she was more involved in the girls' strange behavior than she seemed. The Boits seemed to go through governesses as quickly as painters go through turpentine. Yet Miss Joseph, frightened as she seemed, appeared determined to stay.

I decided to reserve my opinion of Miss Joseph and concentrate on what I had seen for myself. Frightened girls. A hysterical mother. A mysterious light in a mirror. A missing doll. And one whiff of ambergris.

Everything else was hearsay. The rest was nothing, I realized. Nothing I could know was true.

I closed my eyes in weariness, and before them a painting appeared. There was nothing mysterious about it. I had seen this painting often when I was in Spain. Seeing it, studying it, had been part of my reason for going there.

"Visit Spain, Singer," my teacher, Carolus-Duran, had told me. "See all you can of the work of Velázquez. He is my master. In particular, study *Las Meninas*. There is no other portrait like it. Even he never painted such a thing again."

And I had studied it. But why should it come to my mind now, uninvited?

Las Meninas. It had three little girls in it, the young Princess Isabella and her two maids, *las meninas*. But it was no conventional portrait. Velázquez had played tricks with sight lines. He places himself in the portrait, near the girls, looking back at the viewer while he works on another painting. Is he painting you, the looker-on? And the king of Spain is seen in a looking glass, watching the scene of which Velázquez is a part. Through a doorway yet another figure is seen, a nobleman of the court. And a dwarf near Velázquez's feet looks askance at you, the viewer of it all.

What in that painting is the truth? Whose point of view is the true one?

Perhaps Velázquez himself had had something like that in mind, painting the *Las Meninas* as he did. Well, whatever mystery Velázquez had been thinking of, I would use his techniques. The truth about the girls was in the shadows, in the spaces between the figures.

Perhaps what I was drawing there did not wish to be brought to light.

Perhaps light would destroy it, free the children from it. It was at least a possibility.

I would paint the thing itself, if it could be painted. Bring it forth from the darkness. I would pose the girls in the foyer, by the vases, at the edge of Iza Boit's kingdom, as close to freedom as I could bring them. If it did not wish this, let it confront me.

"Let it try to stop me," I said to the empty room.

In The Foyer

I woke the next day excited and happy, emotions I had not felt for some days. I am always this way when I begin a new painting; and in the case of the Boits, I had a special reason for looking forward to beginning my work. I was heading straight for the torpedo line.

I bought ten-foot lengths of good oak for the frame and a huge bolt of plain-weave canvas. I had to hire a wagon and two men to help me with everything, including my sawhorses. The weight of the canvas was so great that it took all three of us to get it up the steps to the Boits' door.

When my helpers had set everything down in the foyer and gone, I spread a ground cloth over the handsome carpet and got to work.

"Would you care for any help at all?" Flint asked me, eying my timber and tools.

"Let me just knock the frame together," I said. "Then I will need some help to stretch the canvas if you don't mind."

Left alone, I looked at the mirror beyond the two immense vases. It looked as bland and ordinary as if it had just come from the factory.

"Well," I announced, "here I am to paint you."

Building the frame took more than an hour. As I hammered and sawed, Flint kept putting his head in to see if I had ruined any of the Boits' treasures with a misplaced blow or somehow slashed the carpet with my saw. But the work went well; and the sounds, and the smell of sawdust, drifted down the hall and up the stairs to the schoolroom.

After a time I looked up and saw Mary and Julia gazing at me. Popau was not with them.

"What are you making?" Mary asked me.

"The frame for the portrait," I said.

"Then what will you do, Uncle Sargent?" Julia asked.

"Stretch the canvas," I said. "A real painter always stretches his own canvas. No shop-bought canvases for me."

"Why?" Julia asked.

"Professional pride," I said. "Anybody can paint a picture. But stretching canvas takes talent. Have you girls been to the Sistine Chapel in Rome?"

"We have," Mary said, "but Ya-Ya is too young to remember."

"I remember," Julia said. "So does Popau."

"Popau wasn't there," Mary said.

I went on. "Do you remember the painted ceiling there?'

"Yes," both girls said.

"Well, the reason Michelangelo had to paint that ceiling was because he couldn't stretch canvas."

They accepted my joke solemnly.

"When I grow up, I will stretch canvas," Julia said.

"And I will come to see your paintings," I said.

The girls went away again and returned with Iza. She was pleased and excited to see the new canvas.

"Mary came and said I must come to see the stretching," Iza said. "She said Uncle Sargent was making the biggest painting in the world."

"I'm glad she brought you," I said, "but I'm afraid I've just finished."

"And where shall I have it set up?" she asked.

"Right here," I said. "In the foyer."

"Here?" she said, and smiled. "But Sargent. Dear Sargent, you're mad. No one has ever had their portrait done in such a place."

She was not smiling now. I could feel my tongue locking up my words. I swallowed and rattled out, "You gave me the idea for it. Seeing your own portrait as Carolus-Duran painted you . . . well, it made me think of the gates of Rome. You as Minerva."

"Of course it did," Iza Boit said. "It was supposed to."

"Well, then," I said. "Here's the next thing. Your girls—not as goddesses, but just as what they are. Beautiful young Americans. No mythology, just—the entrance to a modern home. But—the vases. Tradition, you see?"

I watched her face work. Iza Boit was well pleased that she would remain the only goddess in the family. But the idea of her children being painted here was a bit too avant-garde for her.

"But is this truly the best place?" she asked.

"The light," I said. "At this time of the year, the light is very good here."

"There is other light," Iza Boit said.

"Yes," I said. "The schoolroom has very good light. Shall we work there?"

"So mundane," she said. "So ordinary."

"There is this to be said for using the foyer," I said. "And you have already mentioned it. No one else has thought to have a portrait done in one."

"Very well," Iza Boit said. "Go ahead, Sargent. Let us see what comes of following the ideas of a poor woman hopelessly in love with art."

She was beginning to believe it had been her idea. I sighed with relief.

"I really think the result will be very good," I said. "Perhaps better than you hope for."

"I hope for a great deal from you, Sargent," she said. "And I know I will not be disappointed."

She smiled, and put her hand on my arm.

I flinched at her touch but managed what I hoped was a smile.

"It will be so beautiful," she said, and was off, with Mary and Julia trailing her.

Flint appeared.

As soon as he saw the frame was made, he summoned a maid to sweep up the sawdust. Then he stayed to help me with the canvas.

Understand that this was a bolt of canvas about ten feet long and that I had bought more of it than I needed for this painting. I had another idea in mind for a big picture, and canvas of this kind was not always easy to get. The point is, it was heavy.

But Flint rolled out what I needed—with help from me—almost

as though it weighed no more than a counterpane. And when we stretched it, he pulled it taut with what seemed no effort at all. He was amazingly strong.

When we had the canvas stretched and I had nailed the last corner into place, he helped me to run up the frame that would hold the painting upright. Then he sent for the maid to clean up the new batch of sawdust.

"Flint, you are very impressive," I said. "A painting of this size is hard work. You made it easy for me. Thank you."

"Thank you, sir," he said. "It seemed simple enough."

I was done for the day. Tomorrow I would begin laying the foundation for the painting.

The big white square shone brightly in the pale afternoon light. To my left, down the hall, the mirror caught a little of that light.

"What do you think?" I said to the empty room. "Will it do you justice?"

There was no answer, yet I knew something was listening.

I looked away from my canvas and I saw Florence. She was leaning against one of the huge vases, her body curved so perfectly along it that she and the vase seemed almost to be one thing. She was turned away from me, but she was watching me out of the corner of her eye.

"Hello, Florence," I said cheerily.

She didn't answer. Her silence felt like a challenge. But what sort? And was she the only challenger in that place? What else was watching me?

I began to sing the tune I had been whistling.

"Oh, we'll rally 'round the flag, boys,
We'll rally once again,
Shouting the battle cry of freedom!
Yes, we'll rally once again, boys,
We'll rally once again,
Shouting the battle cry of freedom."

It was one my father had often sung to me during the Civil War, when he had looked west, longing to serve his country but trapped in Europe by fatherhood and his wife.

Florence looked back over her shoulder at me.

"You won't scare anything, she don't care anything," she said.

I decided to try answering her rhyme for rhyme.

"Some creatures of night can be put to flight by the sight of the light," I said.

"Not she, not she. And you will see," Florence returned.

"I want to see. That just suits me," I said.

"But if you do, then she'll see you," Florence said. It sounded like a threat.

"We'll greet each other like sister and brother." I shrugged.

"Oh no, you won't. She's very other," Florence said.

"Let's go to meet her. I want to greet her," I said.

Florence slid away from the vase and disappeared down the hall. I could hardly hear her footsteps.

Looking into the mirror, I sang softly,

"The Union forever,
Hurrah, boys, hurrah!

Down with the traitor
And up with the Star,
As we rally 'round the flag, boys,
We'll rally once again,
Shouting the battle cry of freedom."

Only my own face looked out of the glass at me. And yet I had the feeling something else was in it.

"Am I beginning to worry you?" I asked it. "You should be worried. I'm going to tear you out of this mirror, and out of these girls. I don't think you're nearly as powerful as they believe, whatever you are."

I heard a giggle in the dark. I jumped.

Jane put her head out from behind the other vase.

"You didn't hear me coming, did you, Uncle Sargent?" she said. "I sneaked up on you again."

"Soft as a shadow, silent as a grave," I said.

"Florence walked right past me," she said. "I'm a very good sneak."

"I've never seen a better one," I said. "With a little more practice, you might grow up to be an art thief."

My second joke of the day went off as well as my first.

Jane came toward me and stopped at the opposite edge of the ground cloth.

"I'll bet you don't know what is in these vases, do you, Uncle Sargent?" she asked.

"Miss Joseph?" I guessed.

"Not yet." Jane grinned. "What else?"

"I couldn't say, then," I said. "Darkness, I should guess. A great deal of darkness."

"Yes," Jane said. "It goes on forever."

Again her scimitar smile.

"But it stays in the vases," I said. "Outside, all is light."

"No," Jane said, and spread her arms in one of her graceful dancer's gestures. "It grows and grows. Are you afraid of the dark?"

"No," I said.

"Are you afraid of ghosts?" she asked me.

I don't believe in them," I said. "Do you?"

"I'm not afraid of anything I can kick," Jane said.

"You were afraid of that mirror," I dared. "You could have kicked that."

Suddenly she ran across the ground cloth, took a note out of the pocket of her dress, and pushed it into my hand.

"Tag, you're it," she shouted. Then she lashed out with her foot, kicked me in the shin.

"Damn! That is, ouch!" I said.

"You're stupid, Uncle Sargent," Jane said, and ran off, shrieking with laughter.

I stood there, not knowing what to do next. Was this an invitation to a game? Did she really dislike me? Was it a warning of some kind? What mysterious creatures girls are when they begin to turn into women.

I put the note in my pocket.

Flint appeared and let me out.

Standing on the steps, I unfolded the note, which was written on fine writing paper. I say it was written, but it was not. Instead, the words were made of faint lines cut by a fingernail.

IF YOU DO NOT HELP SOON IT WILL BE TOO LATE
PLEASE
YOUR FRIEND
JANE

I turned and looked back at the door to the Boits' apartment. Such an ordinary door. But what was beyond it?

11

Cloud of Witness

Portraits are exactly like people in one respect. What we see on the surface depends greatly on what is beneath it.

When I begin to paint a portrait, I mix ivory, black, and lead white in linseed oil. I coat my canvas with this until it is a fine gray, like the fog of a spring morning. Then I layer it until I can see into its depth. Then I choose my colors. I know that the gray beneath them will give them an elegant sense of cool, which will please my patrons. That is how they wish to see themselves. But the colors I select are how I see them.

Lilac and lavender are my favorite shades, but they would never do for the Boits. For their young, healthy skins, I chose lead white, vermilion, bone black, rose madder, and viridian green. I decided to paint Florence, Jane, and Julia in black and white school clothes and to give Mary a plum dress for contrast. The only other bit of color I would permit my figures would be a sickly pink ruff for Popau's white dress.

The next day I began laying down the gray. It was a soothing thing to make so many strokes all alike and to see my beautiful fog come into being. I swept my brush strongly across the canvas, feeling like some ancient god creating weather.

The more godlike-playful I felt, the more the things around me began to feel as if they had personalities of their own. It was like slipping backward toward childhood, when one's bed, one's chair, one's plate and bowl all have their own characters. Except that in childhood, these nearly living things are friends.

The things in that foyer were not. The vases stood on guard against me. The red screen pushed me away. The mirror watched. The house was strangely silent. I saw no one in the hall, heard nothing anywhere. Even Flint left me alone. The silence felt like another living presence, and not a friendly one.

Like a frightened child trying to be brave, I began to whistle. Not that I was frightened. Not then.

I worked until my great canvas was a cloud, slowly drying, waiting for what would come next.

A cloud of witness, I thought.

I stepped back and took a look at my work. I would need to put on at least one more coat, but that would have to wait until tomorrow. I was satisfied with what I had, for now. I began to clean my brushes.

The sweet scent of ambergris made me turn my eyes to the canvas.

There, in the drying gray paint, I saw the vague, but real, outline of a form.

It was taller than I was, and its arms were raised high. Whether they were threatening or pleading, I could not tell. The thing had no face, and almost no head, just a mass flowing into the shoulders. I could not see hands or feet; nor could I say if it was male or female. I could not even be sure that it was human. But it was there.

I stopped whistling.

I approached the shape, putting my face almost against it. Up close, it looked exactly like gray paint that was drying a little faster than the paint around it.

I stepped back. The farther I got from the canvas, the clearer the figure became. The edges of the thing seemed to move slightly, even while the shape remained unchanged. Perhaps it was breathing.

"What are you?" I whispered.

And as I spoke, the shape ceased to be. The paint became a uniform shade of gray.

Was I afraid? Yes, but not just afraid. I was fascinated. I felt cut loose from the time and place I was in, even though everything in the foyer still stood out in sharp relief. All of my senses were working together. The scent of paint and ambergris was as immediate as sight, and my ears heard the perfect silence with the attention a fox might give to a rustle in the grass. My skin was alive to the air and to the faint breeze from somewhere that touched my hand. I had the impression that time itself had slowed down, or even stopped.

Not so fast, I thought. I took a crayon and traced the spot where the thing had been. I can't say why I did it. I must have had some thought of catching whatever it was, freezing it in place. Of witnessing it.

It was the work of a moment, and then I had—nothing. A foolish, empty loop—the outline of a child's version of a ghost in a shroud.

"I'm not a child," I announced. "You can't frighten me this way. If you want to scare me off, you'll have to do better."

"I do beg your pardon, sir. Did I startle you?" said Flint.

I could have hugged him, I was so glad to see another person.

"No, Flint, no," I nearly laughed. "I'm just—talking to—to the demons, you know."

"Very good, sir," Flint said. "Would you care for tea?"

"Good heavens, Flint, I had no idea I had stayed as late as teatime," I said.

"It is four o'clock, sir, and Mrs. Boit would not wish you to go without your tea," Flint said.

"Thank you, Flint, I would like some," I said.

"Very good, sir," said Flint. "I'll fetch it at once."

I almost reached out an arm to keep him with me. But the spell, or whatever it had been, was broken. The foyer was empty of feeling.

Flint brought the tea, wheeling a little trolley with a handsome pot, a delicate cup, and a plate of cucumber sandwiches.

Flint poured me a cup, and I sipped. It was good, strong stuff, exactly what I needed.

"Very quiet here today, Flint," I said, studying the outline on the canvas.

"The Misses Boit have gone to Versailles with Miss Joseph, sir," Flint said. "Mrs. Boit is indisposed."

"Any word from Mr. Boit?" I asked.

"A cable, sir, announcing his safe arrival in Boston. Will there be anything else?"

"Yes," I said. "Would you look at the line I've drawn and tell me what it makes you think of?"

"Very well, sir," Flint said, looking at me as if I were being very, very odd.

He studied the canvas intently. He moved closer to it, and to the side.

Then he said, "I confess, sir, it does not make me think of anything. I am sorry."

"No, no, you're perfectly right," I said. "There is nothing there."

"Of course not, sir," Flint said.

Then I said, "Did you smell anything, Flint? When you brought the tea?"

"Yes, sir. The tea. And the paint of course," Flint said.

"Nothing else?" I asked.

"Such as what, sir?" Flint replied.

"Ambergris," I said.

"I do not think so, sir," Flint said.

"Thank you, Flint," I said.

He left.

Alone in the foyer, I finished my tea and cleaning up. It was dark outside now, and the gas lamps had been lit, making the foyer seem warm and welcoming.

When I was about to call for my coat, I walked between the huge vases and faced the mirror.

"I think I like Flint," I said. "I hope he's not helping you. I hope he's an honest man. But what was all this about? Smells and stains on paint. That's all you are, I think. A sort of stain. If you were anything more, you'd do more, wouldn't you? You'd do something horrible to drive me away. Well, I'll be back tomorrow. My canvas will need another coat. I'll cover up that little sketch of mine and go on to paint the girls. And I'll find a way to use this painting to break your spell. You know that, don't you? You know I'm going to win. *Au revoir*."

Flint brought my things. As he helped me into my coat, he said, "I observe, sir, that you have clarified the sketch you asked me about. Though I confess, I don't understand it."

"What?" I said, and turned to look at the canvas.

The figure I had made had altered. The things that might have been arms had extended and acquired hands. The fingers were long, unnaturally long. They seemed to have claws.

"Flint, bring me some bread at once," I said.

"Bread, sir?"

"Yes, soft bread. I use it to rub out stupid ideas. I don't know what I was thinking, Flint. But I don't want the girls to see that atrocity."

When Flint had brought me a fat, fresh loaf, I tore it apart and wadded it into balls. Then I scrubbed them over that lines I had drawn, and the lines I had not drawn.

"There," I said to the empty room once the canvas was blank again. "Much better, don't you think?"

There was no answer, but I knew something had heard me.

12

The Plea

The new strokes of gray went on quickly the next morning, and this time I was not alone. Far from it.

Florence and Jane came silently into the foyer to watch as I started work. They were companioned by Popau, who came cradled in Florence's arms. Florence's eyes seemed turned inward, away from where we were. Jane's face was a study in arrogance.

After they had looked on for ten minutes or so, I said, "Hello, Florence, hello, Jane. Hello, Popau. Did you enjoy Versailles?"

"Too cold, too old," Florence said. "Too many rooms, too many dooms."

"There's a room full of mirrors there," Jane said. "It was too silly."

"So—it was too chilly and too silly?" I said.

"Yesterday. What happened to you, and what did you do?" Florence asked.

"I painted and painted, but I never fainted," I said.

"Did anything dare you, did anything scare you?" Florence said.

"I don't scare so easily, I don't scare so queasily," I said.

"Why do you talk to Florence in rhymes, Uncle Sargent?" Jane sneered.

"Because she talks to me in them," I said.

"I think it sounds stupid when you do it," she said.

"Perhaps you're right," I said. "But I enjoy speaking with Florence however she chooses to talk."

"Do you enjoy it when I kick you?" Jane asked.

"Hardly," I said. "I slept with the light on last night for fear of Jane Boit's big, fierce feet."

"Ha, ha," Jane said. "They're coming to get you."

She came stamping across the floor toward me with her arms over her head.

I backed up, taking us out of the line of sight of Florence and Popau, and anything that might be watching from the mirror.

"Ha, ha," she said loudly, and backed me into a corner.

She kicked me again, in the other leg this time, and shrieked, "Gotcha!"

And from under her pinafore she produced another scrap of paper and dropped it.

"Agh!" I screamed, and covered the paper with my foot.

Florence sidled into view, Popau held before her like a breastplate.

"Come, Jane," she said.

"You're a stupid man, Uncle Sargent!" Jane shouted, and ran to her sister.

They went clattering away.

"This doll is stupid," Florence said, and threw it down at the foot of one of the vases.

I picked up the paper.

STABLES 5
JB
BEWARE F

Stables? There were mews behind the apartments, where the residents kept their horses and carriages. And Jane expected me to meet her there at five o'clock. Or so I guessed. But what did "beware F" mean? Beware of Florence? Why?

I realized then why Jane had slapped Mary that day in the schoolroom. She had been afraid of Florence finding out that it was she who had scratched the first note.

I had thought Jane was the stronger one of the pair. But it was Florence who held power over her sister.

What sort of power?

Perhaps I'd learn something at twilight today.

I finished my work quickly, while Popau looked blankly at the ceiling. I did not hear, see, or smell anything unusual.

When I was done and my brushes were cleaned, I went over to Popau and picked him up.

It was the first time I had ever held him. He was dressed today in a pallid green frock from which his stubby legs protruded stiffly. His pudgy china hands were almost hidden by the sleeves. Above the collar of the dress, his dead white head with its sickly looking pink cheeks and black blank eyes was as bland as always.

I thought that perhaps whoever had made him might once have

intended him for a sailor. That would have made sense for a Cushing child. It was easy to imagine him in a blue suit with shiny yellow buttons and a seaman's beret on his glaring yellow curls. No doubt he had been a fine toy when new. An expensive one.

I wondered which child owner had first dressed him as a girl, and why. Was that what made this expressionless face seem so hideous?

"You're an ugly little fellow, Popau. You know that, don't you?" I said. "When I paint you, I think I'm going to have to make you look even blander than you are. Otherwise you'll draw attention to yourself. And you're only a prop, you know. It's the girls who count, not you."

"I beg your pardon, sir. Are you perhaps finished with the doll?"

It was Flint, of course.

"Oh—uh—yes, yes, certainly," I said. "Miss Florence—just—just—"

"Quite so, sir," Flint said. "But Miss Julia has requested that the doll be brought to her when found."

I handed it over.

"Thank you, sir," Flint said. "Miss Julia will be very pleased."

"Do you find it ugly, Flint? The doll, I mean?"

I don't know why I asked him. Perhaps I just wanted to continue our bit of conversation from yesterday.

"Ugly? I'm afraid I couldn't say, sir. I know little of dolls. But this one seems most important to the family, sir."

"Yes, I know," I said. "Mrs. Boit referred to it as the mystery at their heart."

"Ah," said Flint. "Well, I must say he seems to be a great deal of trouble for a doll. Always wandering off and needing to be searched for. And not very pleasant company when found."

I chuckled, delighted to find that Flint had a sense of humor. I was grateful that he had shared it with me.

Then he said, "I confess I've sometimes had the feeling he is watching me out of those dead eyes."

Flint disappeared up the stairs with Popau.

He returned with my coat and hat, and I went out.

I had several hours before my appointment at five o'clock, so I headed for the bistro where I had stopped a week or so before. The warmth behind the steamed plate glass window was very welcome.

I put my watch on the table before me and ordered. I fear, though, that having a great deal of time to wait, and nothing to read, I had a bit more *vin ordinaire* than I should have had. By a quarter to five I was tipsy, though not drunk.

I hurried to the Avenue de Friedland and up the alley that led to the stables. I stumbled once or twice on the uneven pavement. By the dim light of the houses, I picked my way to the mews belonging to the Boits' residence, pulled my coat tightly around me, and waited.

Somewhere nearby, a horse whinnied inside the warm stables. A cat trotted by, looked me over, decided I wasn't worth running from, and went on its way. The clouds, nearly invisible in the gathering dark, favored Paris with a little snow.

Five o'clock passed. So, I was certain, did five-thirty, though I could not of course see my watch.

I felt my ears freezing. My nose was beginning to run. The wine I had drunk made everything colder.

I began to feel foolish. What was I waiting for, after all? A secret conference with a girl too young to be out after dark? On what subject?

"Sargent," I said to myself, "this could end by being the very scandal your father told you to avoid. Help the children by all means, but on your own terms. Meanwhile, go home."

But I waited a little longer, and at last felt a touch on my arm.

Jane was standing there in a hooded cape that made her look like the priestess of an ancient cult. Or perhaps like Little Red Riding Hood. I could hardly see her, but what little light there was showed me her face, troubled and beautiful.

I had one of my moments of clarity: This girl was not merely frightened, she was lost. She seemed to be floating in darkness.

"I'm sorry you had to wait so long, Uncle Sargent," Jane said. "You know I'm a good sneak, but it was hard to sneak out tonight. Florence is watching everyone. So is Miss Joseph. So is it."

"So is what?" I asked. "Some ghost?"

"I don't know what it is," she said. "I only know what it does. But I don't understand it."

"Can it hear us out here?" I said.

"I don't know," she said. "It can if it's here. But I don't know where it goes. What are you going to do, Uncle Sargent?"

"That depends a great deal upon what you tell me about it," I said.

"It's very wicked when it wants to be," she said.

"It may be wicked, but I don't think it's very strong," I said. "It tried to frighten me yesterday, and all it did was make me look a little foolish in front of Flint. I think it does all it can to scare you because

that is all it can do. Begin to stop being afraid of it, and it will lose
its power."

Jane looked around.

"It wants us," she said. "All four of us."

"But it can't have you," I said. "You know that. That's why you
asked for my help. Because you know I can help."

"Can you help all of us?" Jane asked. "It won't be any good if
you can't."

"Yes, I can," I said. "But before I can, you are going to have to
start telling me everything you know about it."

"Florence knows the most," she said. "All I know is that it's
beautiful."

I pounced on the word.

"What is beautiful?" I said.

"I don't know what to call it," she said. "But you would. You have
to see it."

She would say no more.

"Why did you call me here if not to tell me what you know?" I
asked her.

"To ask you to stay in the house tonight," she said. "Come back
in. Then you can see it when it starts."

"Jane, I cannot possibly come into your home univited," I said. "It
would be very wrong, not to say unpardonably rude."

"I'll hide you," she said. "Please, Uncle Sargent. I can't tell you
what it is. You have to see it."

"Look here, Jane," I said. "This thing you're so afraid of, you say
it wants you. Well, perhaps it can't have you if you don't go to it.

Tonight when it starts, just don't be part of it. Stay in your bed. Put on your light. Don't have anything to do with it. The same for all of you. Start tonight. Resist it and see who's stronger."

"I know who's stronger, " Jane said. "It is. It's very strong."

"Help me, Jane," I said. "Begin tonight. Don't go to it. And tomorrow I will begin to paint you all. And I will bring this thing to light in the painting, and that will help to weaken it, too. It knows this, and it knows that it can't do anything about it. It can't really hurt you unless you let it. Tonight don't let it hurt you."

"Please stay," Jane implored.

"I cannot," I said. "I am a gentleman, Jane."

"Uncle Sargent, we don't need a gentleman," she said.

"Well, I will try to be a hero," I said. "But only during visiting hours. In the meantime, try my idea and see if it helps."

"I have to go back in," she said. "If they know I'm out, something bad could happen."

"Nothing bad can happen unless you let it," I said. "Now, go."

Sadly, her head down, she turned away and left me alone in the dark.

Nothing bad could happen unless she let it, I told her.

What a pompous fool I sounded like.

And she must already have known how very wrong I was.

CHAPTER

13

Miss Joseph

The wild Boits were quiet, waiting, watching. And so was I.

Julia sat on the carpet with a doll between her legs. The doll was not Popau. He was missing. This creature was only there to pose with.

Behind and to her right was Mary, with her hands behind her back and one foot thrust forward. She seemed like a soldier on guard over her sister. Behind them both were Florence and Jane. Florence was lounging against one of the vases, her face in the darkness of the hall. Jane looked straight at me with an unreadable witch-light in her eyes.

And behind them all, the mirror glowed dully with a little reflected light.

I enjoy chatting when I work. It relaxes my subjects and makes the work of sitting easier. If they have friends visit while I am painting, so much the better. It makes for pleasant times.

But the Boit girls had no friends, and today no one was talking to anyone. I was painting stillness. It was not the stillness of deep water, but the stillness of a bowstring taut and ready to be drawn.

Julia was the strangest. She seemed unnaturally calm for a child so young who was made to sit for a portrait. Apart from an occasional glance upward, she was focused on her toy. Perhaps it didn't matter to her where she was. Perhaps she was somewhere else.

This was the more strange because I am not an easy fellow to ignore when I paint. I set the canvas up next to the subject rather than keep it beween us. I stand apart from both, watching. Then when the impressions move me to act, I rush forward, muttering "Demons, demons" or even "Damn! Damn!"

That would never do in the hearing of a child, of course. So I had had a rubber stamp made with the offensive word on it. Smashing it down on a bit of paper over and over gave me much the same relief.

The girls seemed to take as little notice of me as four cats. But, like cats, they were really noticing everything.

Finally, in an attempt to relax things a little, I said, "Let's talk about our favorite places. Tell me, Mary, where is your favorite place in the world?"

Without changing position, she said, "In Mother's room. I like to be there whenever she lets me."

"There's a tree I used to climb," I said. "In Tuscany. A very friend-ly, old pine tree. That was my favorite place."

"Favorite place," Julia said.

"Where is your favorite place, Ya-Ya?" I said.

Julia smiled at me.

"I like to be where P-paul dances."

"Hush," said Mary.

"I don't have a favorite place," said Jane quickly.

Florence whispered something in her sister's ear, and Jane turned white. Florence smiled in a way that was almost evil.

"My favorite place is here. Right here. All year," she said. "But not by the mews. That I won't choose."

"Really, Florence? Why is that?" I asked.

That was the end of that conversation. And my other attempts to begin one were even less successful. I blathered on about my boyhood, my friends, anything. But the strength of their silence grew.

I went on working, and my work went well. I sketched in the lines I wanted and began painting. In a few hours I had made a sort of island of Julia's white dress, her black legs, and part of the carpet where she sat.

Meanwhile, the servants came and went quiet as ghosts.

Finally Flint approached me and whispered, "I beg your pardon, Mr. Sargent, but have you seen Miss Joseph at all?"

"No," I said.

"Well, if by some chance you should, would you please inform me? Mrs. Boit is rather concerned. Thank you, sir," Flint said, and left.

After he was gone, I asked the girls, "You haven't stuffed poor Miss Joseph into one of these vases, have you?"

Jane shook her head slowly.

"Not yet."

That was all the answer I got.

I did wonder for a minute where Miss Joseph might have gone. Perhaps she had suddenly bolted, run away from this strange and terrible place. If so, she would be back soon. I was sure she lacked the courage to leave permanently. And if she had meant to do so, she would have left a resignation.

But most likely she had gone out on some unimportant errand and been detained. That did worry me a little. Paris is not the safest of cities for a young unaccompanied woman. Perhaps she had even meant to meet someone secretly. But that was impossible. The dainty little creature certainly couldn't have a hidden life. Scandal was not only beneath her, it was beyond her.

Teatime came, and Iza Boit appeared. When she saw what I had done so far, she clasped her hands under her chin and announced that the portrait was already radiant. Then she invited me to stay to tea.

The tea was a generous one. The three-tiered serving dish was piled high with cakes and sandwiches.

"Where can that governess of mine have gone?" Iza Boit said. "These children cannot be abandoned like this."

"When exactly did you notice she was missing?" I asked.

"This morning at breakfast," Iza Boit said. "My girls told me her bed was empty."

She did not tell me if it had been slept in, and of course I could not ask. Certainly not in front of the children.

Julia, having eaten her fill of cake, suddenly jumped down off her chair and ran around the room, shouting "Ya-Ya, Ya-Ya, Ya-Ya, Ya-Ya," at the top of her lungs.

"Stay to dinner, Sargent," Iza Boit said. "I have a few friends coming, and I need an extra man."

"Thank you very much, " I said, "but I must go home to change."

"Nonsense. The weather is filthy," she said. "I'll send for your dinner jacket."

"Very nice of you," I said, "but it's several hours until then."

"Let's spend the time looking for my prodigal governess," Iza Boit said. "It will be like hide-and-seek."

This was not what I wanted to do. But how could I say no?

"Very well," I said. "How shall we begin?"

"Come with me and I will show you the apartment," she said. "Even if we don't find a governess or two, you will see some things worth seeing."

Iza Boit led me through the beautiful rooms, pointing out various treasures. If we were looking for Miss Joseph, it wasn't apparent to me. But then, no doubt these rooms had already been searched by the servants. What we were doing was pointless, except that Iza was in an expansive mood and wanted to display the provinces of her empire.

The room that stands out most in my mind however was not part of Iza Boit's realm. It was Miss Joseph's sad little chamber.

Set between the nursery, where Mary and Julia slept, and a large bedroom shared by Florence and Mary, it connected with both, and had just room enough for a simple bed and a small armoire. It was absolutely devoid of personality. Whoever Miss Joseph really was, there was no sign of it here.

I felt like a trespasser, even accompanied by the mistress of the house. Poor Miss Joseph, to have a life so small and barren. Perhaps this was why she remained with the Boits. Because she had nothing else.

As for the girls' rooms, they were magnificently furnished and full of toys, books, and the mysterious things of young womanhood. I recall a rocking horse for Julia that was nearly the size of a cavalry charger, and a bed shared by Florence and Jane that was carved in the faux medieval style that had become so popular recently, hung with red tapestries embroidered with unicorns.

The details of that bed remain fixed in my memory because of what happened next. As Iza was pointing out a small Chinese chest and telling a story about how it had come to the family, we heard a soft, distant scream.

A moment later Flint appeared. He looked frightened.

"I beg your pardon, Ma'am. I believe you should come with me. We have found Miss Joseph."

Quickly, we followed him to the foyer.

All the staff were gathered there, with the girls in a knot beside them. Florence and Jane were clutching each other, and Mary's arms were wrapped around Julia.

"Don't let the children see!" Flint commanded. "Take them out of here."

"But Mr. Flint, they did see," said the cook. "They found her."

"I found her," Mary said. She had tears in her eyes. "We were playing hide-and-seek, and I went behind the screen because I knew Ya-Ya could find me there, and I found her, I found her."

Flint folded back the tall red screen

"Oh, no," Iza Boit gasped, and fainted.

There behind the screen lay all that was left of poor Miss Joseph. Popau lay at her feet. On Miss Joseph's face was a look of stark terror.

Darkness Visible

I stared, stunned at what lay on the floor before me. I was sickened by this thought: Miss Joseph had lain there, already dead, while I painted in this room today. Her sad little body had shown that horrible grimace to the ceiling while I mixed paints and tried to banter with the girls. I felt disgusted with myself.

Flint instructed one of the servants to go for the police. Then the dinner guests began arriving.

Flint turned them away.

"Madame is suddenly indisposed. She very much regrets inconveniencing you, and asks your forgiveness and forbearance."

As for Iza Boit, from the moment she recovered from her faint, she was a whole theater of emotion.

First she screamed. Then she threw her arms around Jane and shouted, "My daughters! My daughters! To have seen such a thing. To have found it. Oh, the horror!"

Then she wept. She almost dragged Jane off her feet with her deep sobs.

Jane pushed her away.

"No, don't. We don't want that."

And Jane hurried away, giving me one tear-filled look.

Next Iza siezed Mary and buried her face in her child's hair.

"My darlings, my darlings. Oh, the scandal. The shame. You will never marry now."

And she wept again.

Then she advanced on Julia, her arms spread and held high above her head.

Julia took one look and bolted from the room, shrieking.

Flint sent a servant to fetch her.

Then Iza turned on Florence, who pushed her so hard that she fell against one of the vases and almost toppled it.

"Leave us alone, ugly crone," Florence shouted.

And she actually took a step toward her mother, copying the arms-high stance that had frightened Julia.

"Monster, you are a monster!" Iza Boit shrieked at her oldest daughter.

"Yes! Monster! Monster, Monster!" Florence wailed. "I am."

And she stalked forward and attacked her mother with her claws. They fell to the floor, locked together, screaming and scratching.

With a look at me, Flint went to separate them. He siezed Iza Boit's arms, and I pulled Florence away.

Florence glared at me silently, then craned her head around me to stare at her mother. There was a satisfied grin on the furious girl's face.

Iza was still shrieking, calling down Biblical curses on her child and demanding to know why she herself was not loved.

"Ma'am, you must do everything you can to compose yourself," Flint said. "The police are coming. If you are calm, they will help you to insure that there will be no scandal from tonight's unfortunate events. You must control yourself."

Iza Boit slapped him.

Not long after the police did come. A detective and a couple of gendarmes. They examined the body and questioned everyone, beginning with Mary.

"How did you come to find the body, mademoiselle?" the detective asked.

Mary explained, pretty calmly, though she made some mistakes in her French. The third time she did so, Iza Boit corrected her.

"Please, Madame Boit," the detective said. "Her grammar is charming. Permit me to take her evidence."

This set Iza off on another tirade. Her daughter's French was and should be flawless, and the police had no right to patronize us.

"Sir, *messieurs*, excuse us, *excusez nous*." Flint said calmly. "We shall return when we are calm."

He picked up Iza Boit by the arms and carried her down the hall, raging at him.

Florence laughed at her mother, then tried to run out the door and was stopped by a gendarme.

The police took it all calmly. No doubt they had seen much worse. One of them took Florence by the arms and held her apart from the rest of us while she raged herself quiet. Another fetched back Jane.

Meanwhile, the detective asked everyone, starting with Jane, what we had seen and heard.

He spoke to me twice. Once along with everyone else and then privately in the grand salon.

The second time was the more interesting. It was then that I realized that I was a suspect.

He began by repeating all of the questions he had asked me before. How long had I been here? Where was I when I heard the scream? What did I do then?

When I had answered, he put away his little notebook and asked me how long I had known Miss Joseph. How well had I known her? What had we talked about? Had we ever seen each other outside the apartment?

I answered as well as I could that Miss Joseph struck me as a frightened young woman who had some kind of attachment to the Boits that kept her here in spite of her fear. I told him what she had told me, which came to nothing, and that we did not know each other apart from this place.

When I was done, he asked me, man-to-man if we had ever met outside the apartment.

"No," I said. "I barely knew the poor woman. I did not quite like her either. I felt sorry for her. But I did not think she seemed trustworthy. Good to the children. I didn't know what to think of her really."

"Nor do I," the detective said. "It would be so much easier to know what to think if there was any sign of violence, but there is none. The young woman seems to have died of fright. And you say she seemed frightened every time you saw her. She would have seemed to want to leave, but she did not."

He had been walking away with his hands behind his back. Now he turned on me.

"You say the Boits seemed to have some mysterious attraction for her, Monsieur Sargent. I suggest it was not so mysterious. I believe she may have been in love with someone and wished to stay near him. Perhaps you."

"Me? Impossible," I spluttered. "If you suspect anyone of that, you had better talk to Flint."

"I believe Monsieur Flint may also have been that man. If there was such a man," the detective said. "Or it may have been Monsieur Boit himself. If this case is still unsolved when he returns to France, we will ask him."

He rubbed his chin.

"Yes. Perhaps this mysterious thing is not so mysterious at all. If Monsieur Boit was the object of Mademoiselle Joseph's affections, perhaps Madame Boit hated her for it. Or perhaps the children did. They all seem rather savage, do they not?"

With a cold thrill of horror, I recalled that day just two weeks past when Jane had introduced her governess to me: "This is Miss Joseph. She is going to die."

No. That was impossible. Whatever this policeman thought, nothing he had said explained what had happened to Miss Joseph. There was another person—or entity—involved. One he did not know about. One I could not even hint at.

"She died of fright," I said. "You said so yourself."

"Yes. I did," he agreed. "But how was the fright prepared and who prepared it?"

He shrugged. It was an elegant shrug. I was sure he practiced it.

"Perhaps the autopsy will tell us more," he said. "There are poisons . . ."

The shrug again.

"And there is something more," he said. "Something you are not telling me."

What could I tell him without sounding like a nervous idiot?

"Sir," I said. "I have answered all of your questions honestly. If you have more questions you have only to ask."

"What do you think frightened Mademoiselle?" he said.

"I do not know," I replied.

"I asked you only for your opinion," he said. "What do you think?"

There was an honest answer I could give, one that would not make me a fool in his eyes.

"I believe she may have been afraid of ghosts," I said. "And I believe she may have thought this place was haunted."

"And why do you think so?"

"For the reasons I have already told you," I said.

"Ghosts," said the detective. "Yes, they are always a possibility. But, I fear, an unlikely one. In any case, Monsieur, I advise you not to leave Paris until this case has been solved."

"I have work to do in the city," I said.

"Ah, your painting, yes," the detective said. "I went to the Salon this year. My congratulations on *Fumee d'Amber Gris*."

"Thank you," I said. "Are you finished with me?"

"For the time being," he said.

I had no intention of leaving Paris, or even of leaving the Boits' apartment that night. If this thing could kill, then Jane and her sisters were in more danger than I had realized. I would have to risk scandal if I was going to help them.

I looked for Jane and found her huddled in the schoolroom with her sisters. One of the maids was with them, a woman who I knew only spoke French.

"I came to say goodnight," I told them. "I can't find Flint. I suppose he's with the detective. Do you know where he's put my hat and coat? They don't seem to be in the usual place."

Jane, who had looked up with silent appeal in her eyes, got up and said, "I know where they are. Come on, Uncle John."

In the hall I whispered, "I'm going to do what you asked. I need you to sneak my hat and coat into Miss Joseph's room later so it will look as though I'm gone. Can you do it?"

"Easy as pie," Jane said. "Thank you, Uncle Sargent. It's very strong tonight."

"Jane," I said, "did it kill her?"

"I don't know," she replied.

I went into Miss Joseph's room and hid myself in the armoire. There was barely room for me, even with my knees up under my chin.

Slowly, I heard the apartment go quiet. The police left. Iza Boit stopped her racket. The girls went into their rooms. Their beds creaked.

Finally, there was silence.

The night was thick and heavy. I cracked the armoire door to let in a little fresh air.

Not long after, I heard someone get up.

I saw Florence pass through the room. She looked ghostlike in her white nightgown. Jane followed her.

"Get up," Florence commanded Mary and Julia.

"We don't want to go there," Mary said.

"I'm sad," Julia said. "I want Miss Joseph."

"It will make us happy," Florence said.

"But then we have to come back, and it hurts," Mary said.

"Someday we will never have to come back," Florence said. "She promised me."

"But then where will Daddy be?" Julia said.

"In Boston," Florence said. "Just like now. Come on."

I heard the other girls slide out of bed. Then Jane came into Miss Joseph's room and beckoned to me.

She passed on into the nursery.

I heard the sound of the girls' feet whispering across the floor. There was a strange rhythm that grew faster and faster. Were they dancing?

I silently unfolded myself and crept across the floor on my hands and knees. I looked around the door.

The Boit girls were twirling silently, with Florence in the middle of her sisters. Like sad, lost planets revolving around a dark star. Each one had one arm extended toward the ceiling and another pointing to the floor.

I knew that pose. It was the dance of the whirling devishes, the Moslem mystics who dance to unite heaven and earth. I'd seen them once on a short trip to Tunis. Where had the girls learned it? Or had they created it themselves?

Was this all that had frightened Miss Joseph? Had she merely been terrified by some slightly wicked game? Then perhaps the girls had killed her with some prank that had gone wrong.

Then I began to feel a change in the darkness, and I knew Miss Joseph had been afraid of much more than what I saw.

As the Boits danced they seemed to be twisting space around them tighter and tighter. No, that was wrong. They were coiling it. Somehow, they were changing something in the air, in the nature of reality itself. I could feel its strength reaching out, touching me.

I stood up.

"Do your damndest," I said to myself, to the night and whatever moved in it.

"She's calling," Florence said, and stopped dancing.

With her arms out before her, high above her head, she walked out the nursery door.

It stood open. It couldn't have been open all this time. But I had never heard it open.

Jane followed her sister, copying her pose. Then went Mary and Julia. I followed.

I knew I was still in the Boits' apartment on the Avenue de Friedland. I could see the walls, the carpet, the doors on either side of me. I knew this. But I also knew that I was somewhere else, that the things I saw had ceased to be real—or at least were no longer the only reality I was in.

We might have been passing through some forest that was ancient when humanity was young. Down some dark mine. Anywhere but where we seemed to be.

We came to the staircase and went down. The girls' feet seemed to be floating, they were so light on the steps.

But a wave of their lonely longing washed back over me. It was in their drooping shoulders, their twisting heads, their outstretched fingers, less than half seen in that terrible night. I could feel a hollow, bitter thing that had no name surround me, and fill me.

How could children bear this? I thought. How long could I? And how did I know so perfectly what the girls were suffering?

At the bottom of the stairs, I felt that like feeling rise up in me. I was sinking into it. It was different from the girls' pain, but part of the same agony. And it was something I had always known was there, though I had never touched it before. New and familiar.

It was a longing, beyond any words, for love. A longing that, I suddenly knew, had driven me to give my life to the painting of beauty. I almost stumbled under the weight of it.

The darkness began to throb with the intensity of our feeling. It was within us and outside us. I could sense it becoming stronger and stronger, though its pulse was below the threshold of hearing.

The foyer gleamed dimly with the light from the street. There was just enough to see the huge Japanese vases, looming larger than ever. Florence stood between them, her arms high and desperate.

"Open, sesame," she whispered.

"Open, sesame," repeated Jane.

"Open, sesame," said Mary.

"Open, sesame," lisped Julia.

Darkness visible. The words, recalled from Milton's description of hell, came to my mind as I stared at the vases, at the girl standing between them.

Was this some private hell the Boits were conjuring? If it was, they were not afraid of it. They copied Florence's stance.

There was nothing around me, nothing beneath my feet. There was nothing but longing. My daylight self was gone, as far off from me as if I were in some other world. And in that moment, all pasts seemed equally likely, all futures equally possible, and all time to be concentrated in one endless moment of need and sorrow.

And in that darkness visible, I saw above us an arch take form, flowing upward from the vases. By some trick of perspective, I saw two heads there, facing in opposite directions. Their eyes were closed, though they smiled down on us. But these were not the faces of Janus. They were the faces of the sphinx.

"The Janus Gate," Florence uttered.

"The Janus Gate," her sisters said.

And then darkness was darkness no longer.

I was no longer in the same place. I did not know where I was, but the light of it grew stronger and more beautiful. I had the impression of—I can't say—temples, fantastic gardens, strange creatures comical and beautiful all around, but without definite shapes. And then, ahead of me, if such things as direction had any meaning, I saw her.

She was dressed all in white, as I had painted her. I could smell the incense rising from before her feet. Her face was turned away, and her strange pale skin seemed to be the source of all the light I saw.

"Come on, Uncle Sargent," Jane's voice said.

The figure turned toward us. She raised her veil above her head and lowered her face slightly to inhale the scent of warm perfume.

"Welcome," she said in the most beautiful voice I had ever heard. "Behold your creation."

15

The Lady of Love

I could only stare. She was the most gorgeous creature I had ever seen in my life. Beauty's fool was pierced heart and mind, and I had no thought of anything until Julia said, "Here is P-paul," and ran to get her doll.

Popau was standing nearby on his stumpy legs with his long white dress tangled around his feet. He held up his arms to Julia, and the dainty Cupid's bow mouth smiled, as it always did.

She picked him up and kissed him. It was hideous.

"Why did you let him come?" Florence asked the exquisite creature before us, pointing at me.

"There are many answers to that," the creature said. "You know one already, don't you?"

"It's because he made you, isn't it?" Jane said softly.

"He didn't make you. We did," Florence said. There was something imploring in her voice.

The creature smiled softly, and took Florence's face in her hands.

"He made me. You make me," she said. "I bless all of you."

Then she turned her eyes on me.

"I have waited for you," she said.

"I—I—you can't—" I stuttered.

"I have waited for you, but it did not seem long. Time does not hang heavy at the Janus Gate."

She took her hands off Florence and reached one out to me. It was cold as ice but familiar as my own skin. And it seemed that I had always known that touch.

"What are you?" I said.

"Who am I to you?" it replied. "I am that, and more."

"You're something I painted," I said. "Your model was an Italian girl. She didn't look like you. She just wore the costume well."

The beautiful face was filled with sorrow.

"And is that what I am?" she said. "Is that really what I am?"

"No," I said. "Not now."

Then she said, "You never named me."

"No," I said. "I never did."

"Do you wish to?" she asked.

"I can't," I said.

To name her was to take responsibility for her. To own her. I could not do that.

"But can we still call you by the name we gave you?" Florence asked anxiously.

"I will be very angry if you do not," she said. "No, not angry. Never angry with my beautiful girls. But I will be very sad."

"The Lady of Love," Florence said.

"The Lady of Love," said Jane, Mary, and Julia.

Around us the light was glowing softer and stronger, pushing back the dark. At the edge of it, I thought I saw trees, trees like the ones that decorated the walls of the foyer, but these were fountains of gold, silver, and diamond. In the center of this mirage, the two great vases seemed larger and more real than before.

"But if this is the Janus Gate, where does it lead?" I said.

"Everywhere," said she. "Forward and backward. Inward and outward. It opens and closes in every one of you. And here all your ways have met."

She took my hand.

"Come, let us walk," she said.

The creature and I led the girls up into a realm of brilliant light. Beyond it I knew the walls of the apartment were still around us, but how far away?

"Uncle Sargent, please don't be silly," Jane said in a voice just above a whisper.

The creature laughed.

"'Tis folly to be wise," she said. "And folly is the greatest wisdom."

The light flickered with all my favorite colors. Lavender, lilac, rose madder, and viridian green came and went like living shadows.

Soon we came to a source of sparks that arced high above our heads and fells into ripples at our feet. It seemed to be a fountain made of light though again, it had no shape.

"Go and drink it," the creature said.

"Don't!" I said, not knowing why I did so.

But Florence skipped to the water and bent her head to it. Jane followed more slowly and cupped her hands, lifting the glitter to her lips.

"Come on, Ya-Ya, let's play," Mary said, and dragged her sister and Popau away.

"Why should they not drink of your fountain?" the creature asked me. "Why should you not?"

"My fountain?" I said.

"Don't you know it?" she said.

She led me closer.

I put my hand down into the ripples. They were as cool and familiar as the creature's touch.

"What is going on here?" I asked. "Where are we?"

"We are where your road crosses theirs," she said.

Then, for just a moment, I was back at the Salon. We all were. Boit was there, holding Julia and Popau. Florence and Mary and Jane were gathered around us, and the angry mademoiselle was still clutching the shoulders of the oldest girls. And yet they were also here, as they were at this moment. And the creature was here and in the painting.

"You all called me forth," she said. "You painted me. They saw me and they sang to me. In their loneliness and sorrow, they found their way through the Janus Gate."

"This is insane," I said.

She took me into her embrace, and I knew that I had always known these arms. Always know them, and been waiting for them all my life.

"You called me forth," she said again. "They called to me. And through them I called to you. Stay with me, John."

My heart leapt like a caged animal trying to get free, trying to open the gate in my heart. I smelled ambergris.

I looked over to where Julia, Mary, and Popau were playing. The doll, stripped of his dress, was stumping across the grass like a clumsy child.

"What is that thing?" I asked.

"The mystery at the heart of us," she said.

That made me angry.

"Tell me what it is," I said.

"What is it? What am I?" the creature said softly. "And for that matter, John, what are you? Do you really know?"

Until tonight I had known exactly who I was. Now, I feared, I did not. But she was not to know that.

"Answer my question," I demanded.

"I don't know what Popau is," she said. "But he helps me. He is my way of touching the place where you are."

"Did you send him to kill Miss Joseph?" I said.

She shook her head sadly.

"No one intended that. Popau frightened her. She found him behind the screen and picked him up. He moved in her hands. She had never seen him move before."

I was sickened by the thought of that ugly little monster, Popau, coming to life; no, coming to—to what? There was no word for it. But acting in the world, luring the girls deeper and deeper into this web of madness. Sweet madness.

"Still, she is dead," I said. "He as good as killed her. You as good as killed her."

"No! Miss Joseph was a sad, lonely girl who was afraid of me because she did not know what I was. She died because she thought I was evil, and she was trying to prevent the girls from coming here."

"But if you are not evil, if I did not threaten you, why did you try to drive me away?" I said.

"I was drawing you to me," she said. "You were intrigued when I tried to frighten you. Do you remember the first note?"

I still had it with me.

DO
NOT
PAINT
BOITS

"I told the girls to write it and have it sent. I told them we must try to frighten you away. But that was not my true desire. I wanted to fascinate you, John. Have I succeeded? Have I transcended that image you painted?"

I did not say anything. I could not.

"I am not wicked," she said. "I only seem wicked where you are. Here, I am as you know me."

"I don't believe you," I said. "What you want for these girls is wrong. Jane knows it. So does Mary. Even Julia is afraid to look at you. You only really have Florence under your spell. I will paint you and break that spell."

"But, John, Master, you have painted me already. That is why I am here," she said.

She was grand and beautiful beyond all telling now. Beautiful and terrible. I said nothing. I had no words.

Every cell in my body cried out for her. Around us, the bright world unrolled farther and farther. I could hear the voices of the girls. Florence sounded happy. So did Jane, now.

"We can stay like this forever?" I asked.

"Forever is so long," she said. "But at the Janus Gate, all time is present."

She kissed me.

Was this paradise, or was this hell? I no longer knew. I only knew that here, now, I was happier than I had ever known I could be.

I put my lips on hers and knew she knew me in all my secret corners. I felt myself falling into her, losing John Singer Sargent somewhere up above.

Over her shoulder I saw Popau in Julia's embrace. He was kissing her.

Goblin and princess.

I forced myself to drop my arms.

"Girls," I called. "Come over here."

They came to me and looked up at us. In Florence's face was a terrible look of hope. Jane seemed balanced between terror and delight. Mary was watching to see what would happen next, and Julia was smiling at Popau.

"May we stay, Uncle Sargent?" Florence asked me.

"Not—not—this time," I said.

The creature turned a sickly shade of green, and her eyes grew hard.

"You belong here with me," she said. "You all do. You know it."

"We belong in the world," I muttered.

"Which world?" she said. "The world of loneliness and sorrow or the world of my love?"

"We can't stay here," I said. "We have bodies. We have real lives. These girls have futures. There is no future here."

"We don't want the future, Uncle Sargent," Florence said. "We want this."

"Uncle Sargent," said Jane, and took my hand.

Mary grabbed the other one. She clung tightly.

"Wouldn't it be nice to stay, Uncle Sargent?" Jane asked, and dug her nails into my hand.

It felt as though she were scratching HELP US into my palm.

The warmth of real flesh gave me strength.

"I have to finish painting you," I said to the girls. "I can't do that here."

"We don't want the painting, Uncle Sargent," Florence said. "The Lady doesn't want it any more. You know that."

"But I said I would," I told her. "I promised your father."

Around us, the shining world began to lose its luster. It was thinning, as if something was seeping into it from the outside.

"Yes, your father would be very upset if I didn't finish painting his girls for him," I said. "He'll be coming back from Boston soon. He'll want to see his girls. We want to make him a picture he'll be proud of."

The light was wavering now. I could catch glimpses of the real stairs, of the real carpet at the foot of them.

"I have work to do," I said. "And so have you. To make your father proud."

I could feel the tension that had underlain the atmosphere all day suddenly release. And the darkness, the real darkness, was all around us.

"If I may inquire, sir, why are you still in the house?" asked Flint.

16

Suspect

We were all standing at the head of the stairs: myself, Florence, Jane, Mary, Julia, and Popau. Flint was at the foot of the staircase, holding a lamp and wearing a dressing gown.

"I was afraid, Flint. I asked Uncle Sargent to stay until we went to sleep," Jane said. "I did fall asleep, and he was getting ready to go; but then I started sleepwalking again. That's what Uncle Sargent says."

Flint's face was as hard as his name.

"Indeed," he said. "Permit me to ask, sir; does Mrs. Boit know that you are here?"

"P-paul knows," Julia offered.

"I am not certain," I said. "I did not speak to her."

I was blushing like my favorite shade of red. I must have glowed in the dark.

"Then perhaps it would be best if you left, sir, and we did not mention this to her," Flint said. "I will wake Madame Brun, the cook, to stay with the children. They are fond of Madame Brun."

"Very well," I agreed.

Neither Mary nor Florence had said anything. Florence did not seem to know where she was. She was looking away from all of us into the darkness of the hall. Mary was still holding tightly to my hand while she clutched Julia with the other. Popau was under Julia's arm.

"Would you care for your coat, sir?" Flint asked. "I am afraid I don't know where it is."

"It's in Miss Joseph's room," I said. "I'll get it."

"Let me go with you, sir," Flint said. "I'm sure you don't want to spend any more time in the dark."

Embarassed as I was, I felt grateful to see Flint coming up the stairs toward me. He was so solid, so real. His light was just a light and not a glittering fountain.

"Thank you, Flint," I said.

"You are welcome, sir," Flint said. "Young ladies, go back to bed."

When I had my coat, Flint led me downstairs.

"Good night, sir," he said. "I trust we will see you again in day-light."

And he closed the door behind me.

I had no idea what time it was. I had no idea how long I had spent at the Janus Gate. Clearly, though, it was late. Nothing was moving on the streets. There were no lights except the scattered street lamps.

I held up my watch to the dim glow and made out that it was twenty minutes after three. There was no way home but by walking. In spite of the danger from late-lurking robbers, I had to do it.

But I saw no robbers. No doubt they were all in bed. I had no company all that long way back to my apartment but the sound of my own steps.

Once, I stopped and listened when I thought I heard someone behind me. Someone walking quietly, but not as an assailant might. These steps were delicate, and I thought I heard the soft swish of a skirt.

I looked back, but there was nothing. I told myself I had imagined it. But I went back the way I had come, just to make certain.

The creature. I had thought it might be she. No, I had hoped for it. She didn't even claim to be real. But the love, the need I was feeling were as real as death.

I knew this was ridiculous, futile. But I also knew we love what we love. I loved the creature. And such a love could only be madness.

I lay awake all night, obsessed by her. When morning finally grayed in the sky, I rose like Lazarus from his tomb, but less lively, and dressed.

I sent to the Boits to ask when I might come to work, but there was no painting that day. Iza Boit was indisposed.

The police came again that morning. The detective I had met yesterday, along with two gendarmes, knocked on my door, and proceeded to question me and my servants for more than two hours.

We went over every detail that he already knew. He subtly shifted his questions, listening for the differences in my answers. Tired as I was, I stammered and contradicted myself enough to condemn me to Devil's Island or the guillotine. But the detective was simply amused.

As he left, he said, "My congratulations, Monsieur Sargent. You are no longer a suspect in the death of Mademoiselle Joseph."

"Have you found your man then?" I said, wondering what he thought he had learned.

"Not yet. But it is only a matter of time. And not too much time either. I believe I may tell you without violating regulations that the butler, Flint, seems to have been Miss Joseph's lover."

"Hard to believe," I said. "Very hard to believe."

I was, in fact, astounded. What could Flint have seen in that shy, frightened little woman? I was almost certain I did not believe it.

But the detective was well pleased with his solution.

"Yes. Servants learn to conceal things well, don't they?" he said. "Of course, they must. They must guard their own secrets, and those of their masters. Good day, monsieur. My best hopes for your future career."

I was left alone.

My thoughts raced over what the detective had told me. Flint was their suspect. And in French law, Flint, once accused, was guilty unless he could prove he was innocent. Poor Flint was in terrible trouble unless I could do something to help him. But what?

I took myself back to bed, determined to get some sleep and go to see my father again. Perhaps he would be able to think of something I could do for the butler.

The one thing that would not help Flint was the truth.

Diagnosis

Mother was disappointed when I arrived at my family's apartment alone.

"Johnny, you promised to bring a friend," she said with a little laugh and a flutter of her hand.

I forced a smile.

"I'm sorry, Mother. Everyone seemed to be busy or out of town. I suppose you'll just have to settle for me."

"Will you stay to dinner at least?" my sister asked.

"I will eat you out of house and home, I promise," I said.

"And leave us to sit alone while he and your father smoke their Havanas," Mother said. "Charming evening."

"Mother, I swear the next time you see me it will be with every American art student I can catch in my net," I said.

"If I cared so much for Americans, I would never have come to Europe, Johnny," my mother said. "Bring anyone, so long as they are intelligent, charming, and single. But no Impressionists. Some of them are not gentlemen."

"And don't bring that Rembrandt fellow either." My sister laughed. "Drinks like a fish and lives with a woman. Scandalous man."

"Emily, for shame!" said my mother.

Father came into the room, carrying a large new book about the Civil War.

"Ah, John, good to see you," he said. "Been reading about our fleet at New Orleans in '62. I'll tell you all about it after dinner."

"Thank you, Father," I said. "But I'd very much like to continue our conversation from last time."

"Oh," he said, "so that matter's not dealt with. Very well."

He went back into his study and put the book away.

After dinner Father and I escaped there and closed the door.

We lit cigars, and our smoke mingled with our silence. At last, my father said, "Which play is it this time? Still *Macbeth*?"

"No," I said. "Stranger than that. More like *A Winter's Tale*, where the statue comes to life."

I told him everything that had happened at the Janus Gate, even the part that was most difficult for me to speak of, the desire I had felt for the creature with whom I had fallen in love.

My father leaned forward as I spoke, his sad eyes locked on mine, his cigar twitching like a compass needle seeking the true north of my story.

When I had finished, he said, "You should leave Paris at once. I will send you word when the Boits have gone."

"I can't do that, Father," I said. "I must help the girls in any way I can."

"I agree," my father said. "And that is the best way to do it. The surest way, at any rate. You must break the connection between you."

"But why?"

Straight through the torpedoes like Farragut at Mobile Bay, that had always been his advice until now.

"Surgery," my father said. "You and those girls together have created this madness. And it is madness, son. Their need for love is so intense, their mother is so heartless, that they have conjured this creature out of your art. Something in your desire for beauty called out to them from the canvas, and together they wove a spell for themselves. A spell so strong that it has drawn you in. It will only grow stronger as they lead you into it."

"I only wish it were as simple as you say," I replied. "But, Father, this creature is not just some fever dream. She's real. To some extent, at least. And so is that damned doll."

"Madness is real," my father said. "Evil is real. And this evil has been manipulating those girls for at least a year. She is manipulating you now."

"She can't control me," I said.

"There is more than one way of controlling someone, John. As I can tell you from my own life."

My father put his hand on my arm.

"With all her creators under her spell, she will be safe and powerful," my father said. "And you will all be mad."

"But Florence is mad now, or close to it," I said. "And Jane knows she will be next. If I do leave Paris, what will happen to them?"

My father did not answer at once. It was not that he did not know what to say. I was certain that he did. But he was a long time finding the way to say it.

"One of the worst things about being a doctor, Johnny, is that there is so much one knows and so little one can do to help."

"But there must be something!" I insisted. "If I cannot help them, you must. You must."

"If you leave, that may weaken her," Father said. "Weaken it. Then when the Boits leave the city, that may weaken it further. But there is no known way to treat most forms of madness. People either heal themselves or they do not."

"Very well, Dr. Sargent," I said. "What is your prognosis? What hope do you see for these girls?"

"I expect this thing will continue its work upon them," he said slowly. "I expect it is too strong to be stopped. I believe it will draw them all into its service and worship. But it must not have you."

"Father, that's not good enough," I said.

"Johnny, there is nothing more I can tell you," my father said. "I don't know what to do. If I did, don't you think I would do it? For their sake and yours? But this web you're in is completely outside my experience. It's outside anything I've ever heard of. Johnny, this thing is like some ancient evil spirit. Something Our Lord might have cast out and sent into a pig. But I can't cast out spirits, Johnny. I can only heal bodies. And as your poor sister proves, I'm not even very good at that."

It was, I think, the greatest sorrow of my father's life that he had strapped my sister to an orthopedic board to straighten her back when she was a baby. It had made her deformity worse. He lived with the idea that if he had done nothing, she would have been better off.

Perhaps that was why, now, he saw nothing to do.

We sat silently for a while. Without speaking, my father trimmed another cigar, gave it to me, and lit it.

We sat together in the smoky room, quiet and very close.

Then as our smokes were burning down to their ends, he said, "You don't mean to take my advice, do you, Johnny?"

"I'm sorry, Father, I can't," I said.

"This creature, whatever it really is now, may be in the process of becoming something else. After all, a year or so ago it was only an image of your own yearning. It existed on a bit of canvas. Now it has a weird sort of quasi-existence in the minds of you and the Boit girls. Who knows what it may turn into?"

"All the more reason not to run away," I said.

My father sighed deeply, rose, and found a red-bound volume in English titled *Folkloric Beliefs of Old Europe*.

"John, you are not being rational," he said. "But nothing about this situation is rational. Therefore, I am giving you this book. It may provide you with something you can use."

"I'll be careful with it," I promised as he handed it to me.

"Be careful with yourself," he said.

18

The Père Lachaise Cemetary

I spent the next three days waiting for word from Iza Boit. The first day, I read the book my father had lent me, looking for clues that might help me to deal with the creature. The second, I sent a message asking when it would be convenient to resume the portrait; but there was no reply. By the end of the third day, I was almost frantic, wondering what was going on among the girls.

It was on the night of the third day that the detective returned.

"*Bon soir*, monsieur," I greeted him. "Am I under suspicion again?"

"Not at all, Monsieur Sargent," he said. "At least, you are not under suspicion of the same crime as before. I am here about a very much more minor matter tonight. What do you know of the disappearance of Flint?"

"If Flint has disappeared, this is the first I have heard of it," I said.

"He has been missing for two days," the detective said. "We believe he realized he was our chief suspect in the death of Miss Joseph, and fled. We are asking everyone who might have known of his plans, or assisted him in any way, to help us. It would be a crime to offer such help or to withhold such information. But you say you know nothing of this."

"That's correct," I said.

"That is very good," the detective said. "The scandal alone of such an act might destroy a man's career."

"Indeed it might," I agreed.

"So I may have confidence that if you should hear anything from the fugitive, you will contact me?" the detective said.

I nodded. I didn't want to speak. To promise in words to betray Flint was more than I could do.

"Very well then," the detective said, "I have your promise, Monsieur Sargent."

He left.

I was sure that the detective was right. Flint had reasoned out that he was the police's favorite culprit and had done something to save himself. He was a resourceful man, and I was sure he had planned his escape as efficiently as he did everything else. But what would he do now? Even if he got out of France, he might never dare to work as a butler again. Any touch of scandal concerning Miss Joseph would ruin him. And of course he could never return to France with any family that might hire him. I almost hoped Flint would contact me. I wanted to help him. And I wanted to know what he knew about Miss Joseph and the Janus Gate.

My thoughts turned to the Boits. Their household must be on the edge of chaos now without Flint to run it.

The detective's visit left me restless. I wanted to do something immediately, and there was nothing I could do. Or, rather, there was one thing, but it was so fantastic, I felt foolish even considering it.

In my father's book of folklore, I had read of a way to summon an unquiet spirit. If one went to a cemetery and walked around it counterclockwise three times, supposedly one would see the spirit coming in the opposite direction. But it must be done at the midnight hour.

It made no sense to do it, of course. But what about any of this made sense? I wanted to see the creature again. I wanted to give her a warning. Either she withdrew from our lives or I would find a way to destroy her. That was what I would tell her.

That was what I told myself.

It was almost three hours to midnight. Plenty of time to get to the Père Lachaise Cemetery.

The gates of Père Lachaise were locked for the night. The black stones climbed the low hill above me like words on a page of a forgotten language. Overhead, the waning moon flickered among the clouds like a dying candle. Its light fell on the monuments, all different sizes, and made them appear to be shifting uneasily in their soil. It was as if they were trying to heave up out of the ground. The tallest ones, statues of iron or stone balancing on plinths of granite, might have been breathing.

If I had wanted to, I could have imagined that the gravestones knew I was there, and were watching.

"What does he want here?" I could have heard them asking each other. "Whom is he trying to call to himself?"

But I pushed such thoughts away. I might be going mad, but I wanted to do so with a clear head.

Feeling foolish and excited, I made the first circuit of the cemetery. I concentrated on my steps, making them as regular as possible. I even counted cadence to myself, as marching sailors would.

"Left. Left. Left, right, left. Left. Left. Left, right, left."

The wind buffeted past me like an army of ghosts hurrying to the sound of trumpets only they could hear.

The second time around, I found the sight of my footprints reassuring. They told me that I was real, that I actually existed. I began my third round feeling almost happy. Either I would encounter something at the end of this business or I would not. Either way, I felt, I would have proved something.

But the weird, tense energy I had felt on the night I went to the Janus Gate grew stronger with every turn around the cemetery.

I tried to whistle "Rally 'Round the Flag, Boys" but it was too cold to whistle. I reached the gates of the cemetery for the third time in silence.

The clouds were over the moon, but the wind carried no sound of footsteps coming toward me. My love was not coming. She was not a spirit, whatever else she was. She had not transformed herself into a creature of myth. She was still a thing of madness. She had great strength, but she was not supernatural.

Then the sky shifted, casting moonlight down onto the thin snow and my black footprints.

Coming toward me I saw Popau.

He stumped slowly, very slowly, between my prints. He fell once.

Then he pushed himself upright and came on, his blind face covered with dirty snow.

I waited at the cemetery gate. When he finally reached me, I said, "What do you want, damn you? I didn't come for you."

Popau's face looked up at me blindly. Then the little monster turned toward the gates. Somehow he climbed them, with his stiff arms and legs clicking against the cold iron. I heard the gate swing open. A narrow gap appeared before me. Popau slid down to the ground and passed inside.

For the first time it occurred to me that whatever force worked inside the doll was immensely strong. I wondered where it came from, what it was. Was it the tool of the creature, or a partner? What made the dark heart beat?

Popau was waiting. Clearly I was meant to follow. I wedged myself between the gates.

Popau led me up the Avenue Principale and off to the left along a curving path. The largest of the tombs bulked against the night like almost-living things. I passed something that might have been a dying lion, and the bust of a woman who seemed to be screaming. Screaming forever in stone.

Our way led uphill to a square monument with a hooded figure on top. Here another road crossed our path.

As we reached the spot, the hooded figure moved.

It was she.

"You have found me, my creator," she said.

"Why? Why here?" I stammered. It seemed to me now that, while I had thought I was summoning her, she had summoned me.

"To show you that the Janus Gate can be anywhere," she said.

She pointed to a nearby grave where something like a sphinx crouched.

I went close enough to read the name beneath it.

"Oscar Wilde!" I said. "But Wilde's not dead. And he's in England."

She nodded.

"He is. And yet he is here as well."

"Then you are showing me the future. Why?" I said.

"I am showing you what is," she said. "When all time is one."

"You couldn't have done this before, could you?" I said, leaning against the tomb that wasn't there but would be one day. "You couldn't have done this before I came with the girls."

"Together we can do anything," she said.

She stepped from the tomb where she stood into thin air. Her veil rippling in the wind, she floated down to the path. But there was no sound as her feet touched the earth.

She came close to me. Her face was more beautiful than it had been before, more beautiful than it had ever been. She was alive, and more than alive; but not in any sense was she human. She was the glory of beauty, of womanhood—its essence.

"The girls," I said. "Where are the girls in all this?"

"They are wherever you want them to be," she said.

Four faint shades seemed to emerge from the night, wavering in the shadows. They did not move. They had no features, no more humanity than sketches. But I knew who they were. I knew that they were waiting.

"Send them away," I said.

"As you wish," she said.

The figures faded out of existence.

I loved this strange creature, whatever she was. I wished only to be with her, forever, at whatever price to my soul, my sanity. But she must not have the girls.

"Take me," I said. "Take me. Let them go."

She laughed, and her laugh was a tiger's purr.

Then she was in my arms, and that was the only reality; and reality seemed to explode within us, around us, and I did not know who or what I was any longer.

When I came to myself again, she was gone. But the scent of ambergris clung to me.

Popau was waiting. Together we left the cemetery. A gray, hopeless dawn was beginning to smear the sky.

We reached the gate, and Popau stepped aside to let me go first. When I looked around, he was gone.

What had I done? What transformation had I undergone? What was John Singer Sargent? Not the same man who had passed through these gates. I had become a lover. Whatever happened next, whatever I decided to do, I was doomed.

19

The Mystery at the Heart

The way home was long, and I took my time. Whenever I saw a café opening up, I stepped in and ordered breakfast. The baskets of bread and the pots of coffee helped me to reconnect with Earth.

My head was whirling. I wanted to follow the creature into what the world would call madness. But I would never surrender the girls to her. But without the girls, would she be herself? Would she be real? And, whatever she was now, what would she become in another day, week, year?

It was midmorning before I turned up the street that led to my apartment.

Marianne, my maid, was furious with me. She could not say so, of course, but she let me know it in the way she sniffed at me and silently took a brush to my clothes.

I went to bed but couldn't sleep. I lay there, electric with tension, fear, and desire. My thoughts followed one another in a circle like hungry wolves: fear of madness, desire for my love, determination to protect the girls. Finally, I got up again.

There was a note waiting for me on the Boits' stationery. I was invited to resume the painting at my earliest convenience.

Immediately I sent back that I would be around at the usual time that day, and got ready.

When I arrived at the Boits' home, it was the footman who let me in.

"I beg your pardon," I asked him as he took my hat and coat, "have you had any news of Flint?"

"I am afraid I can give you no knowledge of that gentleman, sir," the footman said.

The fellow was trying not to smirk. Had he wanted Flint's post so badly?

"I shall miss Flint," I said with emphasis.

"Yes, sir. We all miss Mr. Flint. Madame Boit is most distressed, if I may say so."

Again that smirk, with a little duck of the head.

"Please wait here," he said, and left me.

I had a moment not of overwhelming beauty but of profound shock. I felt sure that Flint had not been Miss Joseph's lover after all. Flint had handled Iza so surely when she raged, picked her up as if she were an angry child. And she has let him do it. No servant—no mere servant—could do such a thing, he would be fired.

I felt sure that Flint had climbed into Iza's bed.

And the servants must surely know it. Did the girls? And if they did, was the knowledge of it pushing them toward the Lady of Love?

But the footman was back.

"Madame will see you in the small salon, sir," he said.

I followed him.

Iza Boit had posed herself for my coming. She had chosen a fainting couch on which to receive me; but she was brightly dressed, and her smile was broad. Her eyes, however, were the same bleak gray as the sky outside, and her flesh was pale.

"Ah. Friend Sargent," she said.

"Mrs. Boit," I said with a little bow.

"I have had a cable from Boity," she said. "He will return home within two weeks. Do you suppose the painting might be finished by then?"

"That's very little time for such a big canvas," I said. "Especially since the girls sit only for brief periods. It might be done, but I doubt it."

"I see," said Iza Boit. "Well, we must do all we can, Sargent. I shall instruct the girls' governess that you are to have all their time until it is finished."

Instruct the girls' governess? I thought. That poor woman was still lying on a slab in the Rue Morgue. What was Iza Boit on about?

"The butler will bring them to you," she said.

The footman, she meant. I saw now what it was she was doing. Iza Boit was not mad—at least no madder than she had ever been. She was instructing me to pretend that nothing that had happened in the last few days had happened.

"Very well," I said. "Shall I wait for them in the foyer?"

"Yes," she said.

And I knew I was dismissed.

The painting still stood in the foyer. Julia and Popau semed to be emerging from a cloud. Or were they being drawn into it?

I turned my thoughts to the creature and to her growing power. I must do something quickly before the misery of the girls' lives overwhelmed them.

When they appeared, they looked as if each of them had taken on one part of their mother's mood and refracted it like a prism. Florence was withdrawn. Jane was arrogant. Mary was afraid. Julia, with Popau, was pretending that nothing was wrong.

I wondered then how I looked to them. How would someone who could see all five of us together paint our portrait? Where would I be positioned among the rest of us? What would my face show?

And there was another presence. Strong and invisible, and as real as any of us.

And not to be mentioned.

Without speaking to me, the girls arranged themselves loosely as I had positioned them for the painting.

I squeezed some colors onto my palette and began to paint. Tired and nervous as I felt, I decided to work only on the darkness at the top of the frame. This was a waste of time, since I didn't need the girls to be there for it, but it was the most I could do.

As I worked, Florence began to rock from side to side, leaning against the vase.

It was as if her rhythm was summoning the creature. And I found my brushstrokes making a kind of counterpoint to the sound of the vase thumping against the floor. And the creature began to emerge from the darkness I was painting, coming in that fragmented way I had sketched weeks ago. But now I knew she was there.

"Oh," said Jane. "Oh. Oh. Oh."

I painted harder and harder, drawing the demon to us.

Then Julia said, "Look Uncle Sargent. P-paul is happy."

I turned to see Popau dancing on the carpet next to her.

Was a dance like this the thing that had killed Miss Joseph?

I put down my brush and watched the damned thing on the floor, stumping through its ugly jig.

Ugly. What we were involved in was ugly. It was mad, and it was cruel. How could I ever have believed anything else?

I looked again at my painting. At the creature there and not there in the shadows,

She had drawn me to her again. She had been drawing me ever since I had met the Boits. And her bottomless need would destroy us all. Popau was dancing her joy. But now I thought I knew how to break the spell she was weaving.

She had said the doll was her way of touching us.

"Yes, he is happy, isn't he?" I said.

I looked out of the window. There were still about two hours of light left.

"Popau is happy, but are we happy?" I said. "Any of us?"

"No, Uncle Sargent," Mary said.

Jane shook her head.

Florence was stone-faced.

"No," Julia said, agreeing with her sisters.

"I think we should all go out with Popau for the rest of the afternoon," I said. "I think we have painted enough for one day, and the light is going to be bad soon anyway."

"Where will we go?" Jane asked.

"On an educational outing," I said. "To a very famous cemetery."

20

Funeral March of a Marionette

Normally it would be impossible for a man to accompany four young ladies without a female escort. But nothing was normal about the Boits.

Iza Boit seemed happy when I suggested that a drive and some fresh air might be good for her children.

Her response, "If the governess agrees," was all the permission I needed.

The footman found the tools I'd asked for—a pick and a shovel—without lifting an eyebrow. I summoned a cab, and the six of us—Florence, Jane, Mary, Julia, Popau, and myself—set out for Père Lachaise.

"Why are we going to the cemetery, Uncle Sargent?" Mary asked me, as we rumbled over the cobbles. She had to shout to be heard. "Is it to see Miss Joseph?"

"No," I said. "But we are going to a funeral."

"We aren't dressed for mourning," Jane protested.

"No warning, no mourning," Florence said.

The noise of the cab made talking difficult enough so that we stopped speaking. I was grateful for that. I didn't want to say what I had to say next too soon.

When we arrived at the cemetery, I paid the cabman and told him to wait. Then the six of us trouped through the gates.

"May I carry Popau?" I asked Julia.

She handed him over.

He was surprisingly heavy, heavier than the other time I had touched him. He hung like lead under my left arm. On my right shoulder I balanced my shovel and pick.

"There are many famous people buried here," I said, as we turned off Avenue Principale in the direction I had gone last night. "It is quite the place to be buried in Paris."

"But why are we here, Uncle Sargent?" Mary asked.

I turned and faced them.

"To bury Popau."

"I was hoping so," said Mary.

"Oh," said Jane. "Oh. Oh. Oh. Yes."

"P-paul?" said Julia.

"No!" said Florence.

Popau stayed inert. I had expected him to struggle, but nothing happened.

"Yes, Popau, P-paul," I said. "We have to do this, not because Popau is bad or because the Lady of Love uses him to do her work in this world, but because we must. We must break the link that binds us to her or become her slaves. She is full of Popau's power. Do you see? If we put Popau underground, then she cannot touch us in this life.

Only if we go to her. And we must never do that anymore. Then we can be—"

Be what? What could I promise them in exchange for destroying their madness?

"Be happy?" Jane said.

"Be free," I said. "Free to be ourselves."

"No," Florence said again.

"Yes, I said. "For you, Florence dear, more than for anyone else."

I put the damned doll down, took off my coat, and began to swing the pick. The iron soil cracked but did not break up into clods. I swung again, and again, until cold sweat ran down my face and hardened in my beard.

"It's cold," Julia said. "Let's go home now."

Mary put her arms around her sister to warm her.

"It's all right, Ya-Ya," she said. "Uncle Sargent will take us all back soon and we'll have cocoa."

"Wicked cold," Julia repeated.

Jane came a few steps closer, fascinated to see the shallow hole finally begin to appear.

Florence stalked circles around me. I thought of the witches in *Macbeth* circling the kettle of evil they had brewed.

"Eye of newt and toe of frog," I chanted to myself in time with the strokes of my pick. "Eye of newt and toe of frog."

As I raised my pick for another swing, Florence darted in beside me and snatched up Popau. She ran off through the cemetery howling, howling as her mother howled.

I ran after her, with Jane at my heels.

Past tombstones and monuments I chased her, with Jane calling after her, "Mumumumum! Mumumumumum!"

I caught up to her beside a towering angel waving a sword. But the sword was broken. The angel would be a weak reed to whatever it tried to defend.

Florence turned and faced me, snarling and grimacing, her back to the grave. She clutched Popau to her like a child she was trying to protect.

I did not speak. I simply held out my hand. When she would not hand over Popau, I took it from her roughly, dragging her down to her knees as she clutched at the thing. She cried, moaned, whimpered all at once.

But once I had the doll, she did not try to get it back. She crouched on all fours like an animal and wept.

Jane knelt beside her and murmured, "Mumumumumum, mumumumum."

I turned away. The cemetery would be closed soon, and I had work to finish.

"Come if you want to," I said.

Under my arm, Popau began to move. He pushed against me so hard that I almost dropped him.

It was obscene, his twisting, his jerking. I could not bear any more of it.

"That's enough out of you," I said, and swung him against a tombstone.

There was no sound but the crack of his china skull on granite, but he struggled harder.

I swung again, and again. Finally I heard his miserable head shatter.

As it did, I felt a surge of energy run up my arms and through all my body. It was the same nervous energy I'd felt at the Janus Gate and on my walk around Pére Lachaise, but stronger, a transforming surge that carried me back to where Mary and Julia huddled in the dark that was almost night now.

"It's cold," Julia said. "I want to go home."

"Just a few more minutes, dear, I promise," I said. And I attacked the ground with all the mad strength that the doll had released into me. The frozen earth parted for my pick, and the shovel gouged out a hole below the frost line. Not very deep, but deep enough, I hoped.

I tossed the headless doll into the little pit and covered it, stamping on the earth and beating it flat with my shovel.

I looked up.

Florence and Jane had come back. They were standing apart from Mary and Julia. They were standing apart from each other. On Jane's face was a look of fascination. On Florence's was a deep, inward despair.

"P-paul is all gone?" Julia said.

"Yes, Ya-Ya," I said. "Popau is all gone forever."

I looked down at the torn earth and hoped to God what I had said was true. I felt the mad energy draining out of me and knew that I would never feel it again. I knew the creature, whatever she had been, whatever she might have become, was gone as well. I knew it as I knew I had two hands, for I felt as though I had cut off one and thrown it into the grave with Popau.

I was free, whatever that means.

A whiff of ambergris came into my cold nose and blew away on the rising wind.

I looked up. The clouds were coming thickly. There would be snow tonight. Snow to cover the deed I'd done.

I picked up my tools.

"Come along, girls," I said. "Chocolate and rolls for all hands."

We left the cemetery just ahead of the closing of the gates.

Homecoming

The rest of the work on the portrait went quickly, in spite of the disorder in the Boit household. The girls, freed from Popau, wandered in and out of the foyer, sometimes willing to pose and sometimes not.

It mattered little by that time; I had their bodies blocked in as I wanted them; and as for their faces, I was no longer trying to paint what they showed the world, but what I saw in them. Jane I put at the edge of the shadow, looking toward me. But still standing next to her, Florence. Which way would she turn? I wondered.

Florence herself refused to speak to me now. She hardly spoke at all. I posed her against her vase, looking toward the mirror, toward the dark that she still wanted.

Mary's face was half in light and half in shadow, with her hands behind her. Strong, stubborn, and secret.

Julia was already finished, but I changed her, turning her face away from the doll that was no longer Popau. I repainted her with her eyes looking off to the side, away from all her sisters, and away from me.

I put in the red screen that had hidden Miss Joseph. I put in the mirror, which now shone with the ordinary light of day.

And in the darkness around Jane and Florence, I painted the absence of the Lady of Love. Whether she no longer existed or simply could not reach us, I had no way of knowing. Nor did I know what I had taken from the girls. I only knew that I had lost the love of my life.

Edward Boit came home a few days before I finished my work. He arrived a day before he had been expected. When he walked through the door, his daughters came running from all over the apartment to surround him. His wife came downstairs slowly, beautifully dressed, making her entrance.

Julia clung to his legs, Mary hugged his waist, Jane and Florence draped themselves over his shoulders.

"Papa's home, Papa's home!" Mary shouted.

"Home, home, home, home," Florence crooned.

Jane only wept.

"Papa, P-paul died," Julia said.

But Boit didn't hear this in the din of his homecoming.

Boit shook off the girls and greeted his wife.

"How are you, my dearest?" he asked.

"We are all very well, Boity." She smiled.

Boit shot me a questioning look. Then he said, "Friend Sargent. I'm so glad to find you here. Let me see the painting if I may."

By now the thing was done except for the lower left corner and part of the right-hand side.

Boit studied it long and thoughtfully while the girls tried to distract him with all kinds of chat and tattle. It was as if Miss Joseph had not died, and Flint had not disappeared, as if nothing that had happened had happened. Except for Boit, they all acted as if I were not there.

Then, after he had rubbed his chin and pulled at his mustache over and over, Boit said, "Everyone go into the small salon. I'll join you there. We'll have a party, eh? Just the family."

They all left.

Boit turned to me.

"Thank you, Sargent," he said.

"I'm pleased you like it," I said.

"It's very skillful," Boit said. "But that was to be expected. No, friend, what I'm thanking you for is showing me what my daughters are living through. I know about the death of poor Miss Joseph. And about Flint's disappearance of course. I'm sure there's a great deal more Iza hasn't told me. When there is time, I'll want a long talk with you about the things that happened in my absence."

"Oh—certainly—yes, Glad to—" I stammered. "Perhaps best if I go now. Family."

I waved my arm in the direction of the small salon.

"I see it all," Boit said, "the shock and fear on the faces of my poor darlings. I will deal with it, I promise you," he said, and squeezed my hand.

He went up the stairs to his family, and I went home, wondering what I could possibly tell Edward Darley Boit that he could believe.

I never did think of a credible tale I could tell him about the things that had happened in his absence, but it did not matter. He never asked.

2 2

Summer

Iza Boit hated the picture I had made. She considered it an act of betrayal. So I was told by mutual friends. She and I never spoke of it. Indeed, for a long time she never spoke to me at all.

I submitted the painting for the Salon of 1881. Everyone said it was very strange, but it attracted just the right balance of approval and satire. It won first place.

With that Iza Boit decided that she had been right all along to hire me and began to let it be known that the composition of the painting had been all her own idea.

The Boits returned to Boston around that time. Boit and I had lunch together several times before they left, but I was never invited to the apartment on the Avenue de Friedland again, nor did I ever see the girls or Iza Boit.

At least there was never a scandal.

I worked, I read, I spent time with friends. Every minute, I longed to see the creature again.

I told myself that that was madness, that I had escaped insanity and had saved the Boit girls from it as well. All this was true, and as the months passed and summer filled France with its green and golden glories, I began to believe these things.

I spent part of that time at the beach, and the light and the wind there cleansed me of regrets and nightmares. The hollow in my heart was still there, but it didn't hurt as it had.

While I was there, I met Judith Gauthier and became friends with her. Judith was a weaver of relationships among the artists and writers who mattered to the art world. She was considerably older than I was; but we had everything in common, and we spent much of our time together.

One day as I was sitting on the beach, watching the waves strike on the rocks and dazzle the air with spray, she called down to me from the dunes. I turned and saw her, and the wind rippled her dress. I had a moment of perfect beauty. It was the first since I had lost the creature.

At last I returned to Paris. While I was certainly not in love with Judith Gauthier, and her age gave me pause, I still thought I might become so, given time.

The evening of the day I reached Paris was soft and blue. It drew me out to stroll the broad ways around the Champs Élysées, simply enjoying the feeling of being back in the most beautiful city in the world. I nodded to every couple I passed, smiling for their happiness and for the hope that was growing within me that I might one day be happy too.

I turned down the Avenue de Friedland and passed the building where the Boits had lived.

In the last light of the day, I looked in at the darkened windows and thought about what had gone on behind them. It was beginning to seem strange, as if it had happened to someone else. Or perhaps in another time, long ago.

I turned back; and as I did, I saw someone in the shadows up the street looking at me. It was only a flash of eyes—sad, angry eyes in an eerie, pale face—and then a lift of the head, a tilt that spoke of absolute disdain, and beyond disdain, self-reliance. Then the figure turned and was gone into the dark.

I ran after it, feeling the same strange energy I had felt each time I had been close to her, but there was nothing to pursue.

I stopped, breathless, feeling my old longing surge back and knowing that time would never heal it.

Above me the sky filled with the bulk of the Arc de Triomphe. It divided the darkening air like a gate. The gate between all pasts, all futures, all possibilities. The gate between this world and the next, where human beings encounter our gods and demons. Between madness and sanity.

I had killed Popau too late. The creature was free of me.

And since that night I ask myself over and over. If she has appeared to me, has she also appeared to the girls? And will they again follow her through the Janus Gate?

And that is all, and not all. This story is still alive in all of us who were touched by it.

As you are an artist of words, I do not expect that these pages of mine will forever remain untransformed by your hand into something perhaps even stranger. I must rely on your own decency to insure that, whatever you make of this, you will insure that the true identities of those involved, persons known to us both, will never be discovered.

The real story must never come to light. Never.

Never.

Never.

Never.

JSS

Sargent's Life and Art

Florence, Jane, Mary, and Julia Boit and their parents were real. There was a doll in the family called Popau or P-paul. The Boits were Bostonian aristocrats who shifted back and forth across the Atlantic at least nineteen times while the girls were growing up. Each time, they took the huge Japanese vases with them.

Not much more than that can be definitely said about the Boits. People guarded their privacy much more closely in those days. A family history says of Iza Boit only that ". . . her eccentricities only made her more charming to those who knew her. . . ."

But it seems clear that there was something about Florence and Jane, at least, that was not right. Whether this was mental or emotional disturbance, the girls grew up into women who were apparently unstable. Mary and Julia remained friends as adults, and Julia became a painter like her father. None of the girls married; but after Iza Boit died, Edward Boit married again and had a second family. Those children did marry and have children of their own.

What Iza Boit was actually like is not knowable at this point;

but when, in 1919, the four daughters donated their portrait to The Boston Museum of Fine Arts, they did so in the name of their father only.

In 1884 John Singer Sargent painted the portrait of Amelie Gautreau, another American living in Paris. Madame Gautreau was a famous beauty of the period who was known for the pallor of her skin. Sargent painted her with her aristocratic profile turned away from the viewer, showing a degree of indifference that, together with the strap of her black dress falling off her shoulder, caused a scandal. In part the scandal was a moralistic one. *Madame Gautreau,* or *Madame X*, as the painting has come to be known, was a sort of creature who had not been seen before in art—a woman of loose morals who was not desperate to please her lover. Beyond this, it has been said, the painting outraged the Paris art world because Sargent and his model had taken everything the French had taught them about elegance and transcended it.

It may be hard to understand such a scandal today, but it was a scandal; and Sargent left Paris to work in England, where his work gradually became less and less daring. After the deaths of their parents, Emily joined him there, and they lived together for the rest of their lives.

Madame X has become an icon of our culture, known to millions of people who have never heard of John Singer Sargent. She seems to have a life of her own.

Like the Boit girls, John Singer Sargent never married. I have tried to make him as close to the living man as I could, but he kept his deepest heart secret.

A Timeline of Sargent's Life

1856 Born in Florence, Italy. John Singer Sargent will live in Italy, France, Germany, and Britain as he grows up. He will speak four languages fluently, and travel widely, but he will always regard himself as an American.

1860 His sister, Emily, suffers the accident that leaves her spine deformed. She is three.

1868 John "is getting old enough to enjoy and appreciate the beauties of nature and art, which are lavishly displayed in these old lands," his mother writes. "He sketches quite nicely and has a remarkably quick and correct eye. If we could afford to give him lessons, he would soon be quite a little artist."

1874 Begins to study portrait painting under Carolus-Duran, France's most popular portraitist at that time. He becomes Carolus-Duran's star pupil.

1880   After a trip to Tangier in North Africa, paints *Fumee d'Amber Gris*, a study of a woman breathing the smoke of an incense that was considered to be an aphrodisiac. His stunning technique and the white-on-white coloring of the canvas make the painting one of the most praised at the Salon.

1882   Paints *The Daughters of Edward Darley Boit*. The painting wins another Salon prize, and Sargent seems on the verge of great success. Sargent once said, "I don't dig beneath the surface for things that don't appear before my own eyes"—a comment that seems mysteriously appropriate for this painting.

Later, Sargent paints *Mrs. Edward Darley Boit (Mary Louise Cushing)* in a portrait of her own. Her daughter Julia gives the painting to the Museum of Fine Arts, Boston, in 1963.

1884   Paints his most famous picture, usually referred to as *Portrait of Madame X*, using Amalie Gautreau, an American living in Paris, as his model. The dropped shoulder strap in the original version, and the fact that Madame Gautreau is apparently dressed only in her underwear, makes the picture too erotic, and there is a scandal that causes Sargent to lose his clientele.

Meets Henry James, the American novelist and essayist living abroad. They become good friends.

1885   Sargent moves to Britain, where he will spend most of the rest of his life. He paints *Carnation, Lily, Lily, Rose*, a sentimental picture of children, to reestablish his reputation as a "safe" painter.

1889   Fitzwilliam Sargent, John's father, dies.

1890   Begins painting a large group of murals, *The Triumph of Religion*, in the Boston Public Library. He has researched this huge project during travels to the Mediterranean, the Middle East, and North Africa. It is a mixed-media extravaganza, with canvas paintings enhanced with plaster, papier-mache, metalwork, cut-outs, glass jewels, and even a type of thick commercial wallpaper that Sargent carves and gilds. He will work on *The Triumph of Religion*, a kind of loose history of religion with an American interpretation, for more than twenty-five years, until 1919.

1906   Sargent's mother, Mary, dies.

1907   Gives up portrait painting. (He will make a few exceptions over the years. Theodore Roosevelt, Woodrow Wilson, and John D. Rockefeller, will be among them.) His famous quote about portraits comes from about this time: "A portrait is a painting with a little something wrong about the mouth." About this time he starts using watercolor more and more, finding it easier to carry the supplies on his many travels.

1907   Turns down a British knighthood because he would have to give up his American citizenship in order to accept it.

1909   Holds a joint watercolor exhibit with Edward Darley Boit at a prominent New York gallery. Of 86 works, 83 are sold. Sargent is one of a number of painters who raise the respectability of watercolor to a level with that of oil painting.

1916-1919   Works on painting, sculpture, and decorations for the Museum of Fine Arts, in Boston, Massachusetts.

1918   During World War I, spends several months on the Western Front studying British troops in the trenches. His most notable painting from this experience will be *Gassed*, a twenty-foot-long picture of sixty soldiers blinded by mustard gas. It is now in the Imperial War Museum in London, England.

1919   The Boit daughters donate Sargent's painting of them to the Museum of Fine Arts in Boston.

1922   Sargent is commissioned to design ceiling panels and murals for the Museum of Fine Arts, Boston, as well as two panels commemorating victims of the Great War at Harvard University's Widener Library.

1925   Sargent dies in his sleep of a heart attack. During his long, prolific career, he created around 900 oil paintings and more than 2,000 watercolors, as well as countless sketches and charcoal drawings. Although his work is dismissed by critics for some years, his reputation rises over the decades.

2004   Portrait of *Robert Louis Stevenson and His Wife*, Sargent's striking portrait of the famous writer, sells for $8.8 million. The painting shows the husband at one edge and his wife, in a golden sari, at the other, with an open door between them. Stevenson said, "It looks damn queer as a whole."

AUTHOR'S NOTE

When my editor, Laaren Brown, suggested that I write a book about John Singer Sargent and *The Daughters of Edward Darley Boit*, she mentioned Henry James's story, *The Turn of the Screw*, as an example of the sort of psychological ghost tale she had in mind.

Doing my research for *The Janus Gate*, I discovered that James and Sargent became good friends a year or so after Sargent finished the painting. It seemed like a good idea to make *The Janus Gate* the story behind the story James would eventually write.

Sargent seems to have been an inspiration to writers. James was to put him into one of his short stories, and in Oscar Wilde's *The Picture of Dorian Gray*, it is a painter based on Sargent who creates the magic portrait that takes all of Dorian Gray's sins upon itself. Wilde's grave is in the Père Lachaise Cemetery, decorated with a mysterious sphinx.

FOR MORE INFORMATION

John Singer Sargent had a long and productive life as an artist, creating landscapes, still lifes, murals, sculptures, and every imaginable type of artwork. But his greatest achievement was surely his portraits. They are considered among the greatest in the history of art, and in *The Janus Gate*, I have tried to capture his thoughts about painting portraits. How much of a person's inner being can be revealed with paint on canvas? *The Daughters of Edward Darley Boit* has made many people wonder. The two older girls—the painting can hardly be called a portrait of them at all, since they are barely visible in the shadows—later, much later, went insane. We have to ask: What did Sargent see in the faces of those girls that made him place them forever in the shadows?

Anyone interested in the real life of John Singer Sargent will find these sources informative.

Books

Davis, Deborah. *Strapless: John Singer Sargent and the Fall of Madame X*. New York: Jeremy P. Tarcher/Penguin Group, 2003.
Although the events described in this book take place just after the period of *The Janus Gate*, this was the most useful book I found for a discussion of the period: the life of upper-class women, the obsession with scandal, clothing, and other things that novelists need to know something about that a biography or history might well overlook. Also the analysis of the elements that made the painting so shocking had some influence on my description of the entity Sargent and the girls create.

Fairbrother, Trevor. *John Singer Sargent: The Sensualist*. Seattle and New Haven: Seattle Art Museum/Yale University Press, 2000.
An analysis of how intensely felt the works of this quiet man really are.

Lubin, David M. *Act of Portrayal: Eakins, Sargent and Jones.* New Haven: Yale University Press, 1985.
This has more information on *The Daughters of Edward Darley Boit* than the other books, but has little to say about what Sargent may be trying to tell us about the girls. Instead, it takes an analytical look at the techniques he used to make this strange painting work.

Olson, Stanley. *John Singer Sargent, His Portrait.* New York: St. Martin's Press, 1985.
The biography gave me the basics of Sargent's life, plus a lot of interesting details that didn't make it into the book: He always wore a suit when he painted and never needed a smock; he ate with his watch in front of him so he wouldn't linger over his food; he collected costumes and played the banjo.

Some websites:

www.abcgallery.com
This is a good website for an overview of Sargent's best-known works.

www.jssgallery.com
A vast resource of all things John Singer Sargent, with a lively community and frequent updates on the latest in Sargent news. It features sophisticated discussions of *The Daughters of Edward Darley Boit*, along with all of Sargent's other major works.

If you would like to see more of Sargent's work, visit some of these **museums and public buildings**.

The Daughters of Edward Darley Boit, along with many other works by Sargent, hangs at the Museum of Fine Arts in Boston, Massachusetts. The website is www.mfa.org. Also in boston, the Isabella Stewart Gardner Museum is home to Sargent's painting *El Jaleo*.

The lady in *Fumee d'Amber Gris* breathes the scented air at the Sterling and Francine Clark Art Institute in Williamstown, Massachusetts. Travel there, or see it at www.clarkart.edu.

Madame X still impresses visitors, though the strap of her dress, once slipping down her elegant shoulder, was repainted in a more decorous position after the first scandal. See her (and other works by Sargent) at the Metropolitan Museum of Art in New York City, or on the website www.metmuseum.org. The Brooklyn Museum in New York is home to *Paul Helleu Sketching*.

The McKim Building of the Boston Public Library is home to Sargent's mural cycle, *The Triumph of Religion*. Recently restored, the murals can now be seen at the library or on a wonderful website, www.sargentmurals.bpl.org. There are more murals at Harvard University's Widener Library, but the library is not open to the public.

Carnation, Lily, Lily, Rose and other works can be seen at the Tate Gallery in London, England. *Gassed* hangs in London's Imperial War Museum.

The Corcoran Gallery, the Freer Gallery, and the White House in Washington, D.C., hold works by Sargent; so do the Carnegie Gallery of Art in Pittsburgh, Pennsylvania, the Armand Hammer Museum of Art at the University of California, Los Angeles, and the Art Institute of Chicago in Illinois. If you live near an art museum, call and ask if you can see works by Sargent there. John Singer Sargent created so much art during his lifetime that there is a good chance you'll be able to see something that sprang from his hands long ago.